# When Night Falls
## Misty Hollow, Book 10

# Cynthia Hickey

For those who love returning to Misty Hollow.

# Chapter One

Delaney Cooper stared at the white sheet of paper taped to the refrigerator. Scrawled was a hurried message from her twin sister, Danica, that stopped Delly's heart.

I've had to run. Got into some trouble that I can't get out of this time. I got rid of my phone so no one can trace me. Don't try to find me, Delly. It's too dangerous. I owe a lot of money to a very bad man and need to go into hiding. I love you. In case of an emergency, you can reach me at the number below. Only in an emergency! Destroy this note.

This was just like Dani. When would she get it through her thick head that someday, maybe this day, she wouldn't come out unscathed from another bad decision? Delly yanked the note off the fridge. Where would her sister go?

Delly slumped against the counter and chewed the inside of her cheek. She could only think of one place. The place their parents always took them on vacation when they were children. Misty Hollow. The town with a lake where their father fished, they swam, and their

1

mother caught up on her reading.

Oh, her mother would be spittin' mad when she found out. How could Dani keep doing this to her family? Well, she'd keep the news from their mother for as long as possible.

She shoved away from the counter and headed to her bedroom, pausing in the doorway of her sister's room. Delly had worked a late shift at the restaurant the night before and hadn't noticed if her sister had even been home. Since her twin wasn't always the neatest, it was hard to tell whether she'd left in a hurry or not. Her room always looked as if a twister had roared through.

Anger rising at all she had to do before she could leave, Delly stormed to her room and tossed clothes into a box to hang up in the camper. Thank goodness, her mother had never sold the twenty-seven-foot camper. Delly would be comfortable enough while searching for Dani even though winter had set in, and Northern Arkansas got much colder than Texarkana.

An hour later, having called work and listened to her boss chew her out then fire her, she backed the camper from the driveway and set off on the four-hour drive to Misty Hollow. She wanted to throttle her sister!

Delly should probably be worried more than mad, but Dani did something like this so often it became a bit like the boy who cried wolf. Most of the time, her "trouble" was greatly exaggerated. Hopefully, this time would be the same. Nevertheless, she had to bring her sister home before Mom returned from her cruise.

After their mother had received a warning not to stress because of her heart, Delly did her best to help her follow the doctor's orders. Dani's actions didn't help.

The forty-year-old camper struggled while going up the mountain, but eventually Delly descended into the valley. She drove at a slow speed down Main Street, marveling at all that had changed in the fifteen years since her family had vacationed here.

A diner looked promising in case it took too long to find Dani and Delly needed to find work. After all, she was out of a job because of her sister. A red-brick sheriff's department drew her attention. Maybe they could help her find Dani. She'd check after settling in at the campground.

Her cell phone rang as she turned into it. Without answering, she climbed from the driver's seat and approached the small building where the site host sat.

"How long you staying?" The old man handed her a piece of paper. "Not many people camp during the winter, so you don't have to rush off."

"That's good. I'm not sure how long I'll be here."

"If more than two weeks, you have to switch sites for another two weeks. If longer than that, you have to pull out for a night before coming back for another two weeks. Can't rent to a squatter."

What a headache. "Thank you."

Her phone rang again as she climbed back into her seat. She glanced at the screen and groaned. Her mother had perfect timing. "Hey, Mom."

"Why won't your sister answer her phone? It goes straight to voice mail."

"I don't know?" She winced.

"Oh, yes you do. Your lies always end with a question mark. Tell me the truth."

"She's run off," Delly blurted. "I'm trying to find her."

"What kind of trouble is she in now?"

"I don't know?"

"Delaney Cooper."

"She owes somebody money. I think she might be in Misty Hollow. I've taken the camper so I don't have to spend money on a hotel room."

"Of course, she went to Misty Hollow. She's always loved that place. Oh, I hope she hasn't done anything illegal."

Delly decided not to tell her about her plan to seek help from the sheriff. "I'll find her, Mom."

"I know." Click.

~

Deputy Joseph Hudson turned from speaking to the department's receptionist as the door behind him opened. A very pretty, very frazzled woman with blond hair cascading down her shoulders stopped and glanced around before approaching the desk.

"Uh-oh." Doris Belwright, the receptionist, shook her head. "I see trouble marching on two legs. Another newcomer."

"Someone new doesn't always mean trouble." Joey chuckled.

"When it's a pretty woman, it does."

"Holler if you need me." He nodded at the woman before heading to the bullpen.

Less than a minute later, the woman stood in front of his desk. "I need help."

"Please. Have a seat." He motioned to the chair across from him. Doris might be right after all.

She sat and set a sheet of paper in front of him. "My sister is missing."

He read the note then straightened and crossed his

arms. "Are you sure?"

"Of course, I am." Her brows drew together. "It says right there that she's in trouble."

"Does she do this type of thing often?" He couldn't help her until he had more facts.

"Yes…but, she's never left a note like this. I'm certain she's in danger." She grabbed the paper off his desk.

"What's your name, ma'am?" He pulled a pencil from a chipped coffee mug on his desk that read, "Life is better fishing."

"Delaney Cooper." She tilted her head. "Are you going to help me or not?"

"First, you need to fill out a missing person's report. If she doesn't show or make contact within twenty-four hours, I'll do some digging." Strangely, the wounded expression on her face tugged at his heartstrings. "Okay, maybe—"

"Hyper on line one," Doris's voice rang through the bullpen.

Joey grabbed the receiver from his desk phone. "Deputy Hudson."

"This is Mrs. Marilyn Cooper."

His gaze returned to the younger Miss Cooper. "How may I help you?"

"My daughter Danica is missing. I want you to find her and bring her home."

He jotted down the daughter's name. "Mrs. Cooper, we have a procedure—"

"Give me the phone." Miss Cooper wiggled her fingers. "Come on. I can handle her."

With a shrug, he handed the phone to her and settled back to watch the show, realizing he might be out of his element with this woman. He smiled at the flush of pink that flooded her cheeks. Her hazel eyes flashed.

"I told you I'm handling this, Mother. You should at least give me some time before giving the deputy a hard time." Her gaze flicked to him. She mouthed sorry.

He waved away her apology.

"This is ridiculous. I'm filling out a missing…because the deputy…of course, I have to do what he says. Mother, enjoy your cruise and let me handle this." She slammed the phone down. "Sorry. She can be a bit…zealous."

"Again, no problem. She's a worried mother. What does your sister look like?"

"Like me. We're identical right down to the long blond hair."

He arched a brow. "How do people tell you apart?"

She sighed. "Danica dresses a bit more…revealing at times, then looks homeless at others. If you see her, you'll know she isn't me."

"Would someone you didn't tell this to know the difference?"

"Maybe not. Does this mean you'll help me?"

"There isn't a lot I can do at this point, but I will keep an eye out for her and ask around town. Where are you staying?"

"Site ten at the campground." She stood and thrust out her hand. "Call me Delaney or Delly. We'll be working a lot with each other."

He returned the shake, enjoying the way her smaller hand fit perfectly in his. "Have a good day, Delaney. Your sister will turn up." Unless Doris was right, trouble had indeed returned to Misty Hollow.

# Chapter Two

Delaney sat on a folding chair, glass of wine in hand, wondering whether the handsome deputy would actually help her. He'd seemed a bit reluctant. Not that she blamed him, not really. In his job, he probably ran across girls like her all the time.

Except this time, Delly's gut told her something was horribly wrong. Their mother felt the same way, or she wouldn't have interrupted her cruise to call the station.

She set her glass on a side table and picked up her phone.

Dani, I need to know where you are.

That was the same type of text she'd already sent five times. Why wasn't she responding? Delly had used the new number her sister gave her.

Her phone dinged.

Stay out of it. I've really messed up this time.

Delly frowned and typed.

Where are you? I'm at the Misty Hollow Campground.

What the heck, Delly? You've brought danger on yourself. These people might think you're me.

No, you brought it on me. Where...are...you? An

icy fist clutched her heart.

I can't tell you. Please go home.

NO.

Then don't blame me when you end up at the bottom of the lake.

I won't. Her sister always jumped in the deep end of anything.

You're so frustrating.

Takes one to know one. Anyway, you know where to find me. I'll keep looking for you.

After several minutes of receiving no more texts, Delly finished her wine and went to bed. She'd pay another visit to the deputy in the morning. After reading the texts, he'd have to see that her sister was in real trouble.

She walked through the doors to the sheriff's office the moment the receptionist unlocked them. "I need to speak to Deputy Hudson. If he isn't available, maybe someone else can help me."

The woman's bright pink lips stretched thin. "He should be here any minute. Please have a seat." She moved to the other side of her desk. "The other deputies are on other business, and the sheriff is off today."

Which was fine with Delly. She'd rather have to convince only one person. To pass the time, she studied the few wanted posters on the wall. Two wanted for murder, one for extortion, and another skipping town on bail. At least Dani's face wasn't up there.

"Miss Cooper?"

She turned to face Deputy Hudson. "Please call me Delaney. Do you have a minute?"

"Of course." He motioned for her to proceed to his desk where he sat, folded his hands in front of him, and set those amazing dark eyes on her. Eyes the color of dark chocolate.

She cleared her throat. "I've received some texts from my sister." She pulled them up and handed him her phone. "Now, will you help me?"

He smiled. "I patrolled the streets yesterday and put the word out for anyone who sees her to contact me." His smile faded as he read the text.

So, he was helping. A load of weight slid from her shoulders.

"She's borrowed money?" He handed her the phone back.

"Yes. Uh...my sister has a gambling problem. Online gambling." Her shoulders slumped. "This isn't the first time she's been in trouble, but it is the first time it's been this serious."

"As in someone after her?"

She nodded. "Most of the time, she spends a night in jail, then gets released."

He turned to his computer and typed. "Quite the petty-rap sheet."

"Embarrassingly so."

"It's not that difficult to tell the two of you apart. She has a different look."

Rough around the edges. World weary. Not taking care of herself. Delly could go on for a while. "What do we do now?"

"Where might she go if she didn't come to Misty Hollow?"

"I have no idea. Texarkana and here pretty much summed up our childhood life. We live together, but my sister sometimes disappears for days at a time. She's never left me a note like this one before." The more Delly spoke, the more worry filled her. What if she really had gotten in over her head this time?

~

Dani should've known her stubborn sister would try and play the hero and come after her. She slammed a glass down on her table at the bar. Too early for alcohol, but after wandering the streets all night, she'd needed a place to sit. Water and coffee would have to be her drinks of choice for the moment.

She also needed a place to stay, but motels weren't safe. Too easy to find her there. What she needed was a vacant building. She had everything she needed. A sleeping bag, toiletries, food and water. She'd be fine for a while. The bad thing…winter was fast approaching. The fog had been so thick this morning she'd almost been run over walking down the highway.

Drumming her fingers on the table, she glanced around the room. No one looked like the type to take in a woman in trouble. Not without benefits, anyway. No, Dani was in this alone.

The campsite drew her. She'd have a hot shower and toilet. Could she pose as a man without her sister spotting her? She could buy a tent and a propane heater. Set up site in the trees and shower after dark. It could work. The campsite was also less than five miles from town, so getting supplies would be easy.

She grabbed her backpack and sleeping bag and headed for the women's restroom. Minutes later, she emerged as a man, her hair stuffed up under a ball cap and her breasts tied down with a scarf. Not even her twin would recognize her at a glance.

The bartender didn't spare her a second look as she left the bar, tossing two bucks on the counter to pay for the coffee. "For the lady in the corner."

"Sure thing, buddy." He kept wiping glasses.

Good. She'd passed the first challenge.

Outside, she called for an Uber to take her to the campground. Dani kept her head down and spoke little. It didn't take the driver long to realize she didn't want to talk. He took her to the store so she could purchase what she needed, then dropped her off at the camp entrance.

Dani approached the camp host and said she planned on primitive camping.

"This time of year?" The man's eyebrows rose. "You'll freeze. There's no sleeping in the bathrooms."

"I have a heater. How much?"

"Nothing. I don't charge crazy people."

"Thanks." Both arms full of supplies and a heavy backpack on her shoulders, she headed for the trees at the back of the bathrooms.

Her gaze cut to her parents' camper. No sign of Delly or her truck. The fifth wheel sat lonely other than a single chair and side table.

After setting up camp, she checked out the bathrooms. Wonderful. They'd been renovated where both the men's and the women's could be locked from the inside. They'd been turned into one big room and were no longer labeled Men and Women. The chance of her running into Delly were slim. Especially since the camper had a perfectly fine bathroom.

Temporary home set up, she darted to the fifth wheel and stole her sister's chair and table. There were others inside for Delly to use. Dani needed a place to sit, and her tent barely had room for the sleeping bag, dollar-store air mattress, and her supplies. The chair and table would squeeze in the corner. She smiled. Looked homey and left her feeling safer than she had in a long time.

Dani curled up inside the sleeping bag and went to sleep.

~

Joey looked up everything he had on Danica Cooper, then knocked on the sheriff's door. "I thought you were off today."

"I am. Needed to get something. What's up?" Sheriff Westbrook closed his desk drawer.

"A woman came to me yesterday and again this morning with concerns about her missing sister." Joey set the printed pages on the desk. "Said she's in a lot of trouble over owing someone money. She seems to think her sister might have come to Misty Hollow."

"Why?"

"They used to vacation here as kids."

"Pretty woman."

Joey grinned. "You should see the twin. Identical, but not. Her sister is more refined. Not so rough around the edges."

"You think it's worth investigating?"

"I do. Something doesn't feel right." Joey gathered up the papers.

"Okay. Spend some time on it until you're needed elsewhere."

"I thought about printing off her driver's license photo and distributing it around town."

"Sounds good." The sheriff waved his wallet. "Can't believe I forgot this yesterday. See you tomorrow."

Joey nodded and headed for Doris. He handed her

the photo. "Can you copy off about twenty of these?"

"Sure. Give me five minutes."

Once he had the copies in hand, he headed for his car. He could only hope that handing out the copies wouldn't alert the wrong person to Delaney. With an untrained eye, the two sisters looked exactly alike.

It would be a pity if she ended up paying for her sister's crime.

# Chapter Three

Delly entered Lucy's Diner and approached the hostess stand. "I'm here about the job posted in the window."

The girl spun around. "Lucy!" She returned her attention to Delly. "Man, I hope she hires you. We're short-handed. Every time trouble comes to this town, people leave."

Before Delly could ask more questions, a woman with bright red hair and a wide grin approached. "Can I help you?"

"I'm here about the job. Is it still available?"

"Absolutely. Do you have experience as a server?"

"For the last ten years." Hope leaped in her heart. If she got this job, she wouldn't have to dig too deep into her savings while she searched for Dani.

"You're hired. Can you start now?"

"I can."

She didn't think it possible for the woman's grin to spread any wider, but it did. "Wonderful. You and our other server, Heather, will be working long days until we can hire at least a part-timer. We're closed on Sunday and Monday. Where are you staying?"

"I've a camper at the campground."

Lucy pursed her lips. "You can park it out back if you'd like."

"That would be great on the day I have to leave, but the view of the lake relaxes me." She couldn't believe her luck.

"Works for me. Come on. I'll find you an apron and introduce you to the chef. He's five-star, but he fell in love with this town and stayed, thank God. My husband sometimes pitches in, but don't tell him that Weston is a better chef."

Delly laughed. "My lips are sealed. Do I have a certain area?"

Lucy made a noise in her throat. "As busy as we're fixin' to be, anyone not waited on becomes yours. Heather and I did the morning shift, you and Heather will do lunch, then you and I will do supper. Come in each day we're open by ten o'clock. Okay?"

"Sounds great. What time does the diner close?"

"Seven o'clock."

Great. She'd have the mornings and part of the evening to search for her sister.

Five minutes later, wearing a ruffled yellow apron with pockets big enough to hide a small dog, she stood next to Lucy who introduced her to the chef, Weston, a handsome man who probably sent a lot of women's hearts fluttering.

"Yes, cute and married." Lucy clapped her on the shoulder then led the way from the kitchen.

"I'm not interested." She didn't have time. Not until things straightened out with Dani.

It didn't take long for the booths and tables to fill. When one emptied, someone quickly took the space. Every stool at the counter was full.

Delly glanced at the specials written on the chalkboard and went to take her first order. Two men in stained coveralls ordered chicken-fried chicken with extra gravy.

"Can't find anything better than Lucy's gravy," one of them said. "You tried it yet?"

"Not yet. Today is my first day." She smiled and turned in the order before taking another one from a couple in a booth by the window.

A young man, slouched over so she couldn't see his face, ambled along the sidewalk across the street. He wore a wool coat that had seen better days, his hands were shoved in his pockets, and his scuffed shoes appeared to be too big for his feet.

Delly frowned. Something about him seemed familiar. She shrugged. Except for the deputy, she didn't know anyone in Misty Hollow.

~

Drat. How was Dani supposed to pick up the order she'd called into the diner with her sister working there?

She couldn't. It looked like there wouldn't be any meals for her that she didn't cook on her propane stove.

A cat darted across the street in front of her. She glanced down the alley it had come from. A man skulked there, then hid behind a dumpster. A cold breeze blew down the collar of her coat, and she shuddered. Whether from the chill or foreboding, she couldn't tell.

Danger was coming to Misty Hollow, and she had brought it here. The danger wouldn't only be to her but to Delly as well. Why was her sister so stubborn as to come after her when she'd asked her not to?

What was their mother going to say when she found out Dani had gotten into trouble again? She should've borrowed the twenty grand from her rather than Oscar Roberto, but she'd panicked when someone claiming to be from the online casino people showed up at her door with the threat of pay up or she'd be sorry.

Dani then went in search of someone to help. Word on the street had been Roberto. Now, look at her. Homeless with a shark after her. The twenty thousand had grown to thirty, and she couldn't see a way out.

~

Joey handed a copy of Danica Cooper's photo to the cashier at the grocery store. "Have you seen this woman?"

Annie Jones nodded. "She was in here buying some groceries just the other day." She peered closer. "Except she looked different somehow. Nicer, maybe."

"You most likely saw this woman's sister. Call the department if you see this one, please."

"What did she do?"

"She's missing." He flashed a smile. "I know it'll be hard to tell them apart, but—"

"I can try." She returned his smile and hung the photo on a board advertising babysitting jobs and pets. "Have a good day, Deputy. I'll call you regardless of which one I see and let you figure them out."

"Thanks." He headed to the mercantile next.

"Sure, I've seen her. She come in and bought a camping chair and table after someone stole hers." Fred Murphy handed him a roll of Scotch tape. "You can tape it up if you want. A customer might mention seeing her, then I'll call you."

He continued delivering the photos, saving the last

for the diner. Everyone had seen Delaney. Everyone in Misty Hollow noticed newcomers, but not Danica. Unless Danica had cleaned herself up. That was a possibility.

The bell jingled over the door of the diner, and he stepped into warmth and pleasant sounds. The murmur of many voices in conversation, the clatter of dishes, the bark of food orders from front to back, and the whine of a small child. Delicious aromas wafted from the kitchen.

Joey shucked his coat and pointed at an empty booth. The hostess nodded and handed him a menu. He waved it off. After all, he knew what he wanted. A bacon Swiss burger.

"Hello, Deputy. Any luck?" Delaney stood, ready to take his order.

"I've distributed copies of her driver's license with private information blocked off, of course." He smiled up at her. "Everyone in town has seen her."

"Really?" Her eyes lit up.

"A cleaner version of her. They've all seen you." He hated the sadness that crossed her face. "If she's here, someone will see her. I'll have the bacon Swiss with fries, please, and coffee."

"Are you going to do anything else besides pass out fliers? She isn't a lost dog, Deputy."

"I know." He wasn't pleased at not having more information for her. "The department is doing the best it can. If she's here, someone will see her."

She exhaled heavily. "I'll turn in your order. Thanks." She turned. The swinging ends of the bow on her apron drew his attention to a nicely rounded figure and long legs. Her wheat-colored hair, tied into a ponytail, bounced past her shoulders. A very pretty woman.

Unfortunately, unless her sister came forward or someone saw her, there was little Joey or the other deputies could do. The woman was an adult. She had every right to go anywhere she wanted.

He straightened when Delaney brought his coffee. "Thanks."

"Your order will be right up." She left to refill the cups of other customers.

Joey sighed and wrapped his hands around the warm mug. He hoped the other twin wasn't in as much danger as Delaney thought. He'd been told Danica often exaggerated, but both Delaney and her mother were worried. Families often had an instinct about danger toward their loved ones that law enforcement might not have.

His order arrived, delivered by a stony-faced Delaney who wouldn't meet his gaze. He sighed again. Anger toward him wasn't anything new to him. A lot of folks thought the department didn't work fast enough.

In small-town America, there wasn't a large law enforcement force. They did the best they could. Misty Hollow had the sheriff, Joey, and three other deputies. All who were keeping an eye out for the missing Danica. At this point, there wasn't a lot more they could do. As awful as it sounded, they needed something to happen in order to move forward.

# Chapter Four

Dani glanced over her shoulder for what seemed like the fiftieth time as she marched down Main Street in the direction of the campground. The man couldn't be following her. No one other than Delly knew about her love of Misty Hollow. Definitely not Roberto.

No, wait, he wasn't actually following her. It was as if he was looking for someone. He glanced up at everyone who passed, stringy dark hair whipping around his face as he slumped against the brick wall of the drugstore.

She shoved her freezing hands into her pocket. A moist mist had settled over the valley bringing a winter chill. What sounded good at that moment was a hot cup of coffee and her sleeping bag.

Thoughts of the warm camper Dani would sleep in that night tugged at her. Even the pullout bed there would be more comfortable than a cheap air mattress children used for swimming. She shook her head. No, she couldn't endanger her sister any more than she already had.

For the first time that she could remember, she wished she and Delly weren't identical twins. If

Roberto's goons did find out she went to Misty Hollow, they could very well try and make Delly pay Dani's debts. They might think she'd made up a fake story about being identical twins to get out of paying. She couldn't let that happen.

At the first sight of him or one of his men, Dani would have to come out of hiding. That would be a horrible day for everyone concerned.

~

Delly glanced out the diner window. A young man in baggy clothes had been loitering by the drugstore for over an hour. He barely glanced up as another young man, hands shoved deep in his pockets, strolled by. Then, he pushed away from the wall and headed toward the diner. She'd seen his type before. Men like him usually purchased a cup of coffee and stayed a while in order to get out of the cold. What was the policy at Lucy's? Were people asked to leave if they hadn't ordered in a while?

She turned her attention back to the elderly couple in the booth in front of her. "What can I bring you this evening?"

"The pork-chop special for both of us." He returned the menus. "No one does a better pork chop than Chef Hoover."

"I'll tell him you said so." She smiled and glanced over when the bell over the front door jingled.

The man who entered froze, his gaze locked on hers, then rushed to the counter and ordered a cup of coffee.

Delly frowned. He'd acted as if he'd seen a ghost.

"Are you okay?" Lucy carried several plates to a table.

"Yes. What do we do about people who loiter—order a coffee and nurse it for hours?"

"Nothing unless we need the stool. Winters are bitter around here, and coffee is on the house when it's cold." She set the plates in front of three men in wool flannel shirts. "Enjoy, boys." She turned back to Delly. "Someone causing you concern?"

"Not yet." She jerked her chin toward the counter.

"Ah. I've never seen him before, but like I said…if we don't need that stool, he can stay." She clapped Delly on the shoulder. "This ain't the big city."

"No, it isn't." Her smile returned as Deputy Hudson entered the diner again. Just about everyone he passed said hello. It was obvious the deputy was well-liked. Once he'd chosen a table with a clear line to the door, she approached to take his order. "I'm sorry for being so touchy with you. It isn't going to be easy to find Danica. What can I get you?"

"The pork chop special, and it's fine. I understand you're worried. I'll be doing another drive around town before heading home after supper. We'll find her. It takes a while to find someone who doesn't want to be found. Since she knows where you are, it's likely she'll come to you."

Delly sure hoped so. She turned in his order. When she headed to another table, the man at the counter turned on his stool, and she felt his eyes on her. He continued to stare as she went from table to table and from table to the kitchen. Did he recognize her from Texarkana?

No time like the present to find out. She moved behind the counter and grabbed the coffee pot to refill his half-full mug. "Do I know you?"

"Nope." He waved a hand to stop her from pouring.

"What brings you to Misty Hollow?"

"Business."

She arched a brow. The torn jeans and coat two sizes too big didn't look like business attire or even comfortable wear for a businessman when the day was done. "What kind of business?"

"You're awful nosy, ain't you?" He scowled. "You don't know me, but I know you, Danica Cooper."

Her heart stopped. "I'm not Danica. I'm her twin sister Delaney. What do you want with my sister?"

"Likely story." He slapped a dollar bill on the counter and slid from the stool. "See ya around, Cooper."

"Seriously. You have me mixed up with—"

He waved a hand over his head and disappeared into the night.

Delly shot a quick glance at the deputy who watched the proceedings with narrowed eyes. Before she changed her mind, she went to tell him about the encounter. "That man thought I was Dani."

~

Joey listened as she told him of the conversation. "I'll see if I can't find him when I finish here. Ask him a few questions." Pretty confident to admit upfront that the dude was looking for Danica.

"What if he finds her before we do?" Delly had paled to the color of parchment paper.

"I'll do my best to make sure that doesn't happen. Why don't you send her a text and warn her that someone is here." He quickly ate, paid the bill, and left. If he didn't see the man wandering around town, he'd check the motel. Misty Hollow only had one, and he doubted the man had driven from any of the neighboring cities.

No, he was searching. Now that he'd found the person he'd come looking for, but he'd stick around waiting for further orders from his boss before confronting Delly again. At that time, he might try to abduct her. The danger to both women just skyrocketed.

After sending the latest information to the sheriff, he backed from the parking lot, cranked up the heat, and cruised the streets at a tortoise pace, his gaze searching the shadows and alleys for anyone attempting to blend in. Not seeing anyone, he drove toward the lake. Might as well check there before the hotel since it was closer.

A young man entered the campground, highlighted by Joey's headlights. Joey slowed, but the guy kept his head down. No long, stringy dark hair fell from underneath the pulled-low ballcap.

Joey parked in front of the campground's host. "Is a thin young man with long dark hair that reaches to his shoulders checked in?"

"Nope. We've got a young man, homeless I think, but he doesn't match that description."

"Thanks." Joey glanced back to where the other young man had gone. No sight of him. "If you see the man I described or a young woman I described the other day, not the one camping here, please call me."

"Sure thing, Deputy. Ain't it something how trouble comes to this town on a regular basis?"

"That's the world we live in. No one can escape it anymore." He returned to his warm car and headed for the Misty Motel.

"Sure, we got someone who matches that description." The manager nodded. "I gave him the key to room twelve. Haven't seen him come back since he left this afternoon, though."

"What does he drive?"

"A beat-up Ford 150. About a 1992 model, I think. Dark blue."

Joey returned to the parking lot. No sight of a truck matching that description. He climbed back in his car and drove to the back of the building. No truck there either. Joey parked alongside the building with a good view of the lot's entrance and settled back to wait. He had no intention of returning home until he spoke to the man.

An hour later, smoke billowing from the tailpipe, a dark blue truck parked in front of the motel.

Joey shoved open his door and headed toward the truck.

The man's eyes widened as he stepped from the vehicle.

"Sir, I'm Deputy Hudson, and I'd like to ask you a few questions."

# Chapter Five

Joey, hand hovering around the gun at his hip, slowly approached the sullen man near the truck. The man's gaze flicked to his weapon. He lowered his hand and repeated that he had a few questions.

"I heard you the first time. Make it quick. It's freezing out here." The man leaned against his truck and crossed his arms.

"Let's start with your name."

"Billy Miller."

"What brings you to Misty Hollow?"

"Business." Miller's lip curled.

"What kind of business?"

"My business." He grinned.

It took every ounce of Joey's former military MP training in order to keep his cool. "What business do you have with Delaney Cooper?"

"You mean, Dani Cooper."

"No, I mean Delaney."

A wariness flickered across Miller's eyes. "Don't fall for her lies, Deputy."

"Maybe you're the one who's misled."

"Are we done?" He pushed away from the vehicle.

"You didn't answer my question."

"I came to deliver a message to Dani."

"How did you know where to find her?"

He scowled. "My boss has ways."

"Who's your boss?"

Miller gave a cocky grin. "Oscar Roberto. Heard of him? Big man. Powerful."

"Oh, I've heard of him. Tell him not to bring trouble to my town." With a sharp look at Miller, he marched back to his car and watched the man enter room twelve. Joey hadn't learned anything Delaney hadn't already told him.

A loan shark was after her sister. He slid into the driver's seat. How in the world had they found out where Danica had gone into hiding?

She'd switched phones, so they couldn't track her that way. Had they implanted something when they'd loaned her the money? He frowned. That was James Bond-type stuff and too far-fetched for him. Easier to believe was that they'd spoken to someone who knew about Danica's love for Misty Hollow, or they'd found something in her home.

He drummed his fingers on the steering wheel. Roberto didn't know about Danica having a twin, so following Delaney's paper trail didn't work. Was it possible the man had enough minions to send him to every city in the state? No. Again, too far-fetched. Roberto had found something to let him think she might be here.

Trouble had again come to Misty Hollow on the trail of a beautiful newcomer. He sighed and drove home. What was it about newcomers arriving that increased the department's workload every single time? Every season, they had a rash of crime to deal with, and it all started with a new woman in town.

At home, he changed into baggy cotton shorts, twisted the top off a bottle of beer, and sat at the kitchen table to plan out how to stop either of the twins from being hurt. First of all, he needed to find Danica. Finding her lessened the danger to her sister...hopefully.

While he didn't want either woman injured, Danica was the one who had made the wrong choice. Her sister shouldn't suffer for her decision to gamble and borrow money.

Second, he needed to keep an eye on Billy Miller. He didn't believe that Delaney wasn't Danica. Things were getting as twisted as a spiderweb.

His phone rang. He glanced at the screen to see Delaney's name. "Hey."

"Hey. Did you find him? The guy from the diner?"

"I did. He still doesn't believe you aren't your sister."

"So, what do we do now?"

"We find your sister. That's the best way to keep you safe." Strange how much he really wanted to make sure she stayed safe, and it wasn't all because of it being his job. Something about Delaney Cooper tugged at him.

"It won't be easy until she wants us to find her."

"Let's hope it isn't too late at that point."

"Deputy—"

"Might as well call me Joey. Like you said, we'll see quite a bit of each other."

"Okay...Joey. Call me Delly. We have to find

Dani before something big happens. How did this man find me?"

"What did you leave back at the house? Papers, anything that might have given them a clue?"

"I don't know. I'll go back on my day off and check."

"Not without me. You can't go back alone."

"Okay. Pick me up Sunday at nine at the campground. Thank you." She hung up.

He smiled at her bossing around a law enforcement officer. Joey'd wager she was the older twin. He finished his beer and tossed it in the garbage, looking forward to Sunday morning.

~

Dani shivered in her sleeping bag, having turned her heater to low. That setting didn't cut through the cold nearly enough. The canvas walls let in too much of the frigidness outside.

The camper where Delly slept would be toasty warm, the bed comfortable under quilts their grandmother had made. Temptation flooded through her. Why did she have to hide in the woods? Why not stay with Delly? She could stay in the camper. No one would see her there. Sure, she'd made a mistake, but did that mean she had to suffer? Delly would want her to be comfortable while they found a way out of her latest trouble, wouldn't she?

Mother must be worried. Oh, she'd be angry since Dani had a penchant for trouble, but she'd still worry about her until she heard from her. Wasn't it selfish not to relieve her mother's worry?

Excuse after excuse flooded through her as she continued to shiver. Winter had only begun in the mountains. It was insane to think she could survive the coming months in a tent.

The more the cold seeped into her bones, the more tempted she was to go to the camper. The only thing holding her back was the fear of endangering her twin. Surely, there was a way to keep them both safe and Dani out of the woods.

She reached over and turned off the heater, giving in to the temptation. Unzipping the tent's opening, she crawled out, dampening the knees of her sweatpants. Straightening, she studied the dark area. No one moved at this time of the night. Heck, there were only three campers, and one belonged to the host, the other to Delly. Who would be dumb enough to stroll the campground when it was this cold?

Pulling her coat tighter around her, she dashed for her mother's camper.

~

Why was someone hammering at ten p.m.? Delly hugged a pillow to her ears. The pounding continued. After several minutes, she realized someone was knocking on the camper door. Her heart beat in her ears. Only bad news came at night. She tossed aside the heavy quilt and slipped her feet into fuzzy slippers. As she passed the kitchen counter, she grabbed a knife from a drawer and peered out the window.

A young man in a baseball cap and wool coat pounded on the door. She recognized him from the sidewalk across from the diner. Her hand tightened on the knife. The man stood on tiptoes and peered in the window.

A shriek escaped Delly.

The man removed his cap. Long blond hair fell

past his shoulders. Dani!

Delly shoved the knife back in the drawer and yanked the door open. She reached out and pulled her sister inside. "You're crazy, you know that?"

She shrugged, unbuttoning her coat. "Can I stay here? A tent in the woods is too cold."

"You were in a tent?"

"Yeah. Behind the bathrooms." She tossed her coat onto a chair. "We can talk more in the morning. Make some plans."

*Just like that, her sister returns and starts making demands.* Delly crossed her arms. "I don't know if I want you here."

Dani toed off her boots and pulled out the sleeper sofa. "Do you have enough blankets? I'm not kidding. I'm freezing."

"Did you hear what I said?"

"Yeah, but you don't mean it. Where are the blankets?" She started opening cupboards.

"Stop. They're under the bed." Shaking her head, Delly pulled out two blankets and tossed them at her sister before handing her a pillow. "We will definitely be talking in the morning. You'd better not run off."

"I won't." Dani stripped to her underwear and burrowed under the blankets. "It's too cold for that."

"Well, thank God for winter." She stormed back to bed and tossed and turned for the next hour before sleep finally overtook her. Her anger toward Dani hadn't dissipated during the night. Not even the smell of cooking bacon could soothe her emotions. "Well?" She glowered at her sister from the bedroom doorway.

"Geez. Let's at least eat first. Have you talked to Mom?"

"Of course. She's already terrorized the sheriff's department about looking for you."

Dani laughed. "Sounds like her."

"This isn't funny." She slid into the booth. Let her sister do the cooking and cleaning. She owed Delly that much, at least.

"I saw you working at the diner." Dani scooped some scrambled eggs and bacon onto a plate and set it on the table in front of Delly. "Do you work today?"

"Yes. I'm off on Sunday and Monday." She sprinkled salt and pepper over her eggs.

A couple of minutes later, Dani slid across from her with her own plate. "I guess you have a lot of questions."

"Obviously, I know what you put in your note and in the texts. How did this happen?" Appetite gone after a couple of bites, she set her fork on her plate.

Dani sighed. "I lost a lot of money gambling and borrowed thirty-thousand dollars. Well, actually twenty, but he said I have to pay back thirty. I don't have that kind of money."

"You should've thought of that before gambling it away. What happened to your job? Couldn't you have started saving? Pay in installments?"

Her sister's face reddened. "I'm a year late in paying."

"A year?" Delly bolted to her feet. "Mom is going to have a fit."

"I know." Her voice was hushed. "I just can't help myself. I need professional counseling."

"Don't go and try to make me feel sorry for you, Dani. This is big trouble, and you've got me involved." She told her sister of the man approaching her in the diner.

Tears sprang to Dani's eyes. "That was never my intention."

"It never is. I have to get ready for work. What are you going to do?"

"Stay here. If I do go out, I'll dress as a guy again."

Delly exhaled heavily and closed the pocket door of the bathroom area so she could shower. Normally, she'd head for the public shower building but didn't relish going out into the cold, misty morning on a short night's sleep.

When she'd finished and dressed, she found her sister still at the table with an empty plate in front of her. "The least you can do is clean up."

"I've been thinking."

Uh-oh. "That is never a good thing coming from you."

Dani glanced up. "I'm going to borrow your clothes. There are going to be two Delaney Coopers. If we look the same, and the sheriff's office continues to say you aren't me, and we never are seen together, it might work."

"And then what? It all goes away?"

"You receive news that I'm dead. Car wreck, drowning, suicide, I don't care, as long as Roberto thinks I'm dead."

Delly shrugged into her coat. "It might actually work. I'll see if Joey…Deputy Hudson is willing to play along. If he presents me with something saying you're dead in front of that guy, it might work."

"Joey, huh?" Dani arched a brow and grinned.

"It isn't like that. We're simply working together."

She opened the door and glanced over her shoulder. "What about next time, Dani? You going to gamble under my name? Because I won't let that happen."

# Chapter Six

Joey knocked on Delly's camper door and stepped back when she answered. "You ready?"

A sly smile graced her lips. "Sure. Come on in."

He narrowed his eyes and climbed the steps. Something seemed off about her, but he couldn't put his finger on it. Until he stepped inside. Two identical twins, almost identical to his trained eye, smiled at him. "So, you came out of hiding?"

"Can you tell who is who?" Delly asked.

He nodded. "There's a hard gleam in your sister's eye that you don't have."

Dani frowned. "Really?" She shrugged. "Oh, well. It was worth a try."

"I doubt anyone else can tell. I'm trained to notice the small things." He glanced at Delly. "Are you ready?"

"Yes." She turned to her sister. "Stay inside, Dani. We can't risk it. If someone sees me with the deputy, then sees you out walking the streets, the ruse will be up."

The cloudy look on the sister's face said all Joey needed to know. She didn't like being ordered around. As soon as he and Delly were out of sight, she'd be in town. He could only hope she didn't raise suspicion. It would be better for both women if those hunting Dani thought only her sister was in Misty Hollow. "She'll be out that door in minutes." He opened the door of his truck for Delly.

"Yes." She sighed. "It's nice seeing you out of uniform."

"It's nice being out of uniform." He grinned and started the engine. "Ready to do some searching?"

She nodded. "We need to know how that man found Dani."

"We will." Eventually. Either they'd discover how, or the man would let them know. Joey hoped for the first option.

"We have a few hours' drive. What do you want to talk about?" He cut Delly a glance. "Makes the time go by faster than silence."

"Okay. You first. Why a deputy?" She turned sideways as much as her seatbelt would allow.

"I'm former military police. Seemed like a logical job choice."

"Why Misty Hollow?"

He smiled. "That question will answer itself when you've been here a while. The beauty and the people get under your skin. At least for those native to the town or those who have been here for a long time. The people are friendly and always willing to lend a helping hand. Trouble always comes from the outside."

"Like with me."

"Yeah." He hated to agree with her on that point, but she was right. "Have you always been a server?"

"Since high school. Turns out I'm good at it. I like people and it shows, which results in decent tips." She glanced out the window. "This is a beautiful mountain, but I don't intend to stay any longer than necessary. My home is in Texarkana."

Her remark landed like a lead balloon in his gut. "Family there?"

"My mother, once she returns from her cruise."

"Right. I remember her."

Delly laughed. "She's hard to forget. Don't be surprised if she shows up here if this whole thing lingers. My mother will turn your beloved town upside down. She's...like a twister. An F5 when she wants something."

"Which means she'll make things worse."

"Absolutely. I love my mother, but yeah...it's best we stop this before her cruise is over."

"When's that?"

"Next weekend."

He seriously doubted they'd know anything definite by then. Misty Hollow needed to prepare for a storm named Marilyn Cooper.

~

Dani watched the truck leave the campground, then slipped her phone into the pocket of the jeans she wore and stepped outside, pulling the camper door closed behind her. She smiled at seeing Delly's truck. Her sister always left the keys in the sun visor. Too trusting, that one.

Dani needed a place with a strong Wi-Fi. If she could win at online poker enough times, she might secure the money needed to pay off Roberto. She had five hundred dollars in the bank. All she needed now was luck.

Hard gleam? She frowned at the deputy's

description of her. What did he expect from someone who had lived a hard life? Things didn't come as easy for Dani as they did for her sister. All her life she'd had to study harder and work harder. A girl needed to play, didn't she? That's what poker did for her. It gave her a high nothing else could. Sure, she'd been told to seek professional help, but why? All she needed was a big win, and all her problems would be solved.

Dani drove to the local library and chose a table in the back where she wouldn't be disturbed, then connected to the free Wi-Fi. Taking a deep breath, she opened the gambling app and bet a hundred dollars, doubling her money in the first two hands. This was more like it.

Three hours later, she'd doubled the five hundred to a thousand. She could do this. It would take a while, but luck was with her today. She set her phone down. Since she was ahead, maybe she should stop and try again tomorrow. After all, she didn't want the luck to run out. But then, if she could increase the winnings up to ten thousand, Roberto might accept the money on faith she could repay the rest.

She drummed her fingers on the arm of the chair. The responsible thing to do would be to pretend to be Delly and go to the diner and work for the tips. It would take years to earn the amount she needed, but it would put money in her pocket so she wouldn't have to touch what was in the bank. That money was for Roberto. After thirty minutes of tossing the idea around, she headed for the diner.

A woman with bright red hair glanced over. "You're off today, Delly."

"I know." She flashed a grin. "I was bored and

hoped you could use the help. And I could use the money." She noticed the apron the other server wore.

"Absolutely. I'll take however long you want to give me."

Someone called for Lucy, and she rushed away.

Dani smiled and headed for the back to grab an apron.

~

Delly unlocked the door to the house she shared with her sister. "Mom lives in a condo. She said she wanted her privacy."

"Do you think anyone could have gone to her place and found out where Dani went?"

His question made her steps falter. "I...don't know. Maybe we should go there when we're finished here." Wouldn't someone have contacted her if her mother's place had been broken into? "Mom would have photo albums of our trips there."

"Where do you want to start?"

"Dani's room. Everything she has is in there. It's my house. She lives with me and tells me all the time how I make her feel like a renter because I harp on her to clean her room." She shoved open her sister's door.

"I can see why. Is this normal?"

The room looked as if a bomb had gone off. "Yep. It would be hard to tell whether someone had ransacked the place. Start digging. I'll take the closet."

"I'd rather take the closet." Joey stepped ahead of her. "I don't like rummaging through a woman's undies." He winked. "Unless...well...you know."

Mercy. Her face heated. "Good point." She cleared her throat and opened the first drawer.

An hour later, they hadn't found anything that

mentioned Misty Hollow. "Maybe she accidentally mentioned the place to Roberto."

"Maybe." Joey closed the closet. "After checking out your mother's place, how about we grab a bite to eat before heading back?"

"Sounds like a great idea." Her stomach rumbled in response. "Or eat first?"

He laughed. "We can eat first. Where's a good place?"

"There's a family-owned restaurant that serves American and Mexican food. You're bound to find something you like."

"It isn't hard to please me food-wise." He placed a hand on the small of her back as if he'd always done it.

Electricity rippled up her spine. A very long time had passed since a man had touched her even if Joey didn't mean anything by the act. Outside, she stepped away from him and locked the door before sliding back into the passenger seat of his truck. "I really hope today isn't a waste of time."

"It isn't. I'm enjoying spending the day with you." His smile warmed her face and her heart.

Good grief. She acted like a silly teenager and didn't say anything on the drive to the restaurant out of fear of saying something stupid. They weren't on a date. They were trying to help Dani. Now was not the time for romantic ideas.

At the restaurant, Joey opened the door for her, letting her step inside ahead of him. "Is everything okay?"

"Sure. Just thinking about all we have going on." She hoped he couldn't tell she was lying.

"Okay." He held up two fingers to let the hostess

know how many were in their party, then followed Delly and the hostess to a booth.

The girl handed them both menus and took their drink orders, promising to return soon to take their order.

"I love the chimichanga here." Delly browsed the menu, knowing she'd order the same thing she did most of the time. "The bacon Swiss mushroom burger is to die for. That's what I'm ordering."

"Make that two," he said as the server set their sodas in front of them. "I never can turn down a good burger."

"What if we don't find anything at my mother's?" She removed the paper wrapping from her straw.

"I plan to keep talking to the new guy in town. Hopefully, he'll tell me something eventually. I don't think he's going anywhere until he finds your sister."

"Which will be harder if we can't convince him she isn't there."

"Even harder if he insists you're Dani. That's the scenario I really don't like." He reached over and put a hand over hers. "I'll do my best to keep the two of you safe, Delly."

"I know you will."

They ate quickly, not wanting their trip to Texarkana to take the entire day, and she gave him directions to her mother's. "She has a ton of nosy neighbors who will think I'm bringing a boyfriend by."

"Let them think that." He flashed a grin. "Imagine your mother's surprise when she comes home and hears the stories."

Delly shoved her door open. "I have a key to the back. Fewer spying eyes." She led the way through a gate into a postage-stamp sized yard and froze. The arcadia door sat open, a nice sized hole in the glass where someone had broken in.

# Chapter Seven

Thank God, her mother wasn't home. If she had been, whoever entered without permission would've ended up with a skillet upside the head. Delly took a step closer to the door.

"I'll go first." Joey pulled a gun she didn't know he had from under his shirt. "Stay outside."

"No way." She grabbed the tail of his shirt and held on so he couldn't get away from her. Her heart drummed in her throat. What if whoever broke in was still inside? Her palms grew sweaty. Sure, Delly had come to Misty Hollow to save her sister, but in reality, she was nothing more than a great big chicken. She'd come to bring Dani home, not face off with ruthless people.

Maybe Dani had exaggerated. Maybe she had made things sound worse than they were.

Joey stepped inside, glass crunching under his feet. He glanced over his shoulder and put a finger to his lips.

Did that mean…A scuff sounded down the hall. Yes, someone was inside. Her grip on Joey's shirt tightened.

"You're choking me." His whisper sounded way

too loud. "You should stay outside."

"Sorry, not a chance." She released her grip and wiped her sweaty hands on her jeans.

Gun at the ready, Joey moved at a snail's pace down the hall, placing each foot as if he thought he might give them away by stepping on a twig. Not that Delly was in any hurry to face whoever was back there, but the anxiety had her stomach roiling.

A muffled thud broke the silence as if something dropped. A short curse. Delly's legs trembled. She should've waited outside as Joey had suggested, so she turned to head back.

A man passed by the kitchen window. They were surrounded.

She tapped Joey's shoulder and pointed.

He grabbed her hand and pulled her into the bathroom, closing the door except for an inch to peer out.

Delly stayed so close to him his body heat warmed her cold hands. She peeked under his arm.

The second man didn't make any attempt to be quiet. He marched down the hall as if he owned the place. As he passed the bathroom, she recognized him as the man who had approached her in the diner.

"Hey, Steve. You find anything yet?"

"I don't even know what I'm looking for. Quiet down, or a neighbor will hear us and call the cops."

"You're looking for any sign that there are twins." Billy called him an idiot, then headed past the bathroom again.

They'd have their answer soon enough once they looked through her mother's photo albums. Then what? Did that increase the danger to Delly? Now that Dani had decided to dress like her, no one except Joey would be able to tell them apart. That made a high chance they'd both be taken and made to pay. The man, Roberto, might think Delly owed him the same as her sister did.

As she and Dani were growing up, they often got into trouble together or pretended to be each other so often that no one believed either of them was good. But Delly had *always* been the one who followed the rules. Still her rowdy sister convinced everyone otherwise. This situation might not be any different. Her mouth dried up at the thought. How were they going to get out of this alive?

Her phone rang.

Joey gasped, then grabbed her hand again and flung open the bathroom door. Without a word, he dragged her at a sprint toward the sliding glass door.

"Hey." Billy tried blocking their way.

Joey slammed his shoulder into the guy and kept running, not releasing Delly's hand.

A gunshot rang out behind them, which must have shattered one of the wine bottles in her mother's wine rack. She shot a quick glance to her right. Burgundy liquid spilled down the cabinet like blood.

More gunshots rang out as they careened around the corner of the building and dashed for the truck. Delly scrambled inside as Joey dove into the driver's seat. Before she had her seatbelt on, they were rocketing down the road while he shouted into his radio.

She put her seatbelt on and stared out the back window. "They aren't chasing us."

"Good." He didn't slow their speed. "Answer that

phone before I toss it out the window."

"Oh." Fear had blocked out the sound of the jazz music she'd set to let her know when her mother called. "Now is not a good time, Mom."

"I'm calling to see whether you've found your sister."

"Yes, I have. She's staying in the camper with me."

"Then, the two of you can go back to Texarkana."

"Uh…"

"What?" Her mother's voice rose an octave.

"Someone broke into your house and shot at us when you called me and gave away our hiding place."

"I'll be on the next plane home. If I have to, I'll book a helicopter." Click.

"Uh-oh." She glanced at Joey. "My mother's coming home early."

"That's going to make things tough. I don't take her as someone to sit back and let the authorities do their job."

"You'd be right. She'll insist on interfering." She stared out the passenger-side window, her heart rate returning to normal. "She'll try to tell you how to do things."

"I think I can handle your mother."

Two squad cars, lights flashing, zoomed past them on the other side of the interstate. Delly straightened in her seat. "Should we go back?"

"No, I'm not putting you in anymore danger. I'll file a report at the office. The Texarkana PD can handle those two, if they're still there. Which I doubt. Want to stop at the diner for a late supper before I take you to the campground?"

"Sure." Although, after the day they'd had, she didn't know if she could eat a bite.

Dusk had settled by the time Joey pulled the truck into the parking lot of Lucy's diner. By then, Delly's stomach rumbled. A bowl of hot soup with a hearty slice of homemade bread sounded perfect.

"You okay?"

She frowned. "Why wouldn't I be?"

"You probably haven't had many afternoons like we just did." He held the door open for her.

"True. But, we made it out of there without a scratch." Thankfully.

He smiled. "You were great. Very brave."

"Hardly. I wanted to throw up." She grinned back and stepped inside.

Her gaze clashed with her sister's.

Heads turned.

Gritting her teeth, Delly marched across the room. "What do you think you're doing?"

Dani shrugged. "Making some pocket money?"

Lucy stepped from the kitchen. "A lot of things about today make sense now." She shook her head and delivered plates to a nearby table.

"You should've told me." Delly crossed her arms. "Now you've blown our story. Everyone in town now knows there are two of us."

"Maybe that's just as well." Joey motioned toward an empty booth. "You couldn't keep it a secret forever."

"Ugh." She plopped into the booth. "I love my sister, but I don't want to pay for her choices."

~

The bell jingled over the diner entrance.

Joey glanced toward the door as Billy and another guy strolled in, both carrying guns. He moved his hand slowly toward his weapon.

"Don't even think about it, Deputy, or I shoot someone. Steve, go secure the back door. Hey, redhead. Come lock this one."

Lucy glared at him but locked the door.

"Now pull the blinds down."

She did as told.

"Anyone with a gun, put it on the table in front of you, and my buddy will gather them. Anyone tries something dumb, someone else dies. Their blood will be on your hands. Red, go fetch the chef and anyone else in the kitchen. I want everyone where I can see them."

Joey set his gun on the table.

"We'll need that," Delly hissed.

"I'm not going to be responsible for him shooting someone. Don't worry, I'll figure something else out." It wouldn't take long for the sheriff's department to find out they had a hostage situation on their hands.

The man named Steve returned with two women who had been hiding in the restroom, and Lucy returned with her chef husband, Greg. Hoover must have had the night off. Lucky man.

Joey rubbed his hands down his face. It had been a long day, and there didn't seem to be an end in sight.

"You twins, get up here by the counter." Billy waved his handgun. "Come on. Make it quick."

Delly gave Joey a wide-eyed look, then slid from the booth and joined her sister at the counter.

"Okay, people. Take a good look. One of these women, maybe both—" Billy gave an exaggerated shrug. "Owe my boss a lot of money because of gambling debts. Now, which one of you is Dani?"

Delly linked arms with her sister and hiked her chin. "You'll have to figure that out."

Joey's heart stopped as the man aimed the gun at her head. He started to get to his feet only to have Billy swing the weapon his way. Hands up, Joey sat back down.

Billy's attention returned to the twins. "You have exactly ten seconds to tell me which of you is Dani or I shoot someone."

With an audible exhale, Dani unlocked arms with her sister and stepped forward. "I'm surprised you couldn't tell. After all we've been through together." She crossed her arms and leaned against the counter. "We had something once, Billy. You going to throw that away?"

"I work for Roberto, and I do what he tells me. Where's the money?"

"I'm working on it. I only have a thousand, but I'll get the rest. Promise." She reached for him.

"Not good enough." He stepped back, then glanced around the room. "Maybe you can persuade these nice folks to pitch in donations." His brows raised.

"I'm not going to do that."

Red and blue lights flickered through the blinds. The cavalry had arrived. Things would either get worse or better now.

Lucy and her husband moved to stand in front of Joey's table. A Glock stuck out from the man's waistband.

All Joey needed now was the opportunity and the chance to take Billy down without anyone else getting hurt.

"Release the hostages, and come out with your hands up," the sheriff's voice boomed through a horn.

"Everyone line up in front of the windows. Now." Billy waved his weapon while Steve blocked the hall leading to the restrooms. "Until Dani figures out how she's going to pay back my boss, no one leaves."

Joey sighed. It would be a very long night.

# Chapter Eight

Roberto scowled at his phone as Steve rambled on about a full diner and the sheriff's department. "I don't care. Get me the girl or my money. Preferably the money."

"She has a thousand."

"Take that. Tell her she has one week to find the rest, and I'll be coming to get it myself."

"But...what about law enforcement outside? Billy and I can't come out of this alive."

"That's your problem. Have the girl wire me the thousand. Figure out the rest yourselves." He hung up and stared out the window of his New York penthouse. "I hate fools."

Most people were expendable. Like the two idiots he'd sent to search Misty Hollow. A drunken Dani had spoken often about her love of the town, so it was the logical place to look. Stupid girl never remembered conversations after having too much to drink.

A pity, really, that it had to come to this. Beautiful, even if she wasn't that bright. He'd offered her the option of being his mistress. Something she'd flatly refused. Seemed she had some scruples after all.

"Oscar?" His wife entered the room. "The cook

says dinner is ready."

"I'll eat in my office." He turned, brushed his lips across her cheek, and headed for the one room that belonged only to him. The one room his wife and daughter were not allowed in. Someday, Jessica, his daughter, would overtake his business since he didn't have a son, but at the age of eighteen, she'd need to wait until after college.

"Daddy?" As if his thoughts had conjured her up, his daughter hovered in the doorway of his office with a silver tray in her hands. "Here's your dinner. Filet tonight." Her lips curled into a smile, then faded. "Trouble with work?" She lowered her voice. "Someone not paying up?"

Shock reverberated through him. "What do you know about that?"

She gave a humorless laugh. "I'm not as naïve as Mother. I know how you put a roof over our heads."

"Who told you?" His blood boiled.

"Just pillow talk, Daddy." She set the tray on his desk. "And, I don't kiss and tell. Not when my father is so ruthless." She reached over and patted his cheek. "I'm ready to start my training any time."

"Finish college first." He'd kill the fool who told her before he was ready.

"Don't growl. You can teach me on my breaks. I don't return to college until next semester, remember? I finished my courses early." She sat without being invited and crossed long legs.

He stared at her plain face wondering why she hadn't turned into the beauty her mother was. Any of his men spending time with her only did so to get close to him. Or…marry her and gain an empire when he died. It definitely wasn't because of her beauty or personality.

With a sigh, he dug into his food.

~

"Roberto says to wire the thousand right now." Steve stood in front of Dani. "You have one week to come up with the rest, and he's coming to collect it personally."

How in the heck was Dani going to get twenty-nine-thousand dollars in a week? She swallowed past a desert-dry throat. "Okay." She fished her phone from the pocket of her apron and transferred the money. Except for the fifty dollars' worth of tips she'd earned, she was officially broke. "It's done."

Maybe if she recanted on Oscar's offer of her being his mistress, he'd wipe away her debt. Could she, though? The man was married. Dani hadn't stooped so low yet as to have an affair with a married man. For the first time since becoming addicted to gambling, she'd ask her mother for a loan. At least if she couldn't pay her mother, her life wouldn't be in danger.

Delly's shoulder pressed against hers. Her trembles shook Dani's arm. This was Dani's fault her sister was held hostage. Her fault these other people were in possible danger. "I'm sorry, Delly." Tears stung her eyes. "I'll get help, I promise."

"I've heard that before." Her voice shook.

"I know." She took her sister's hand. "We'll be okay." *Please, God.*

~

Delly glanced at the stony-faced Joey who had yet to move from the booth. The chef and Lucy stood in front of the table where Delly had sat. Despite the fear rippling through her, she narrowed her eyes. What were they up to? Hopefully, it wouldn't result in anyone dying. "I'm going to throttle you when we get out of here." She tightened her grip on Dani's hand. "I thought it was scary at Mom's condo when I was almost shot, but this is a hundred times worse."

"Someone tried to shoot you?" Dani's eyes widened.

"These two goons." Slowly, as the two men continued to converse by the register, Delly's fear started to subside. Maybe they'd take everyone's money and move on, now that Dani had sent some money to their boss.

Slipping her hand free of her sister's, she tiptoed back to the booth. No one in the room made her feel safer than Joey.

"You okay?" He studied her face as she slid in across from him.

"Yes." Her gaze landed on the gun in the chef's waistband. Ah. Joey was waiting for the right moment to take it. "Why is the sheriff holding back?"

"He's waiting to see what the two men will do." Joey took both her hands in his. "You're cold."

"Just...nerves. It's been quite a day."

He chuckled. "Yes, it has."

"Will it be a long night?"

"Most likely."

Delly groaned and rested her head on her folded arms. *Come on, Sheriff Westbrook. Do something.* She looked back up. "What's your plan?"

"Don't have one. I'm going with the flow. If Billy or Steve try something, then I'll act, which could get someone hurt or killed. I'm trying to avoid that from happening."

"Okay." Made sense. Her gaze fell on an elderly lady sitting alone at a table near the kitchen. The unfolding events didn't seem to faze her as she sipped tea and read a book. "Who is that?"

"June Mayfield. It's rare that she ventures out of her home."

"I'm going to check on her." Helping others would relieve some of her own anxiety.

"Ms. Mayfield? May I?" She motioned to a chair across from her.

"Of course." She smiled. "You're the reason we're here, if I heard that man correctly."

Heat rushed to her face. "Well, my sister is. You seem awfully calm."

She shrugged. "It's for this very reason I rarely leave my house. I decided to eat someone else's cooking for a change. I'm too old for this world, my dear. There are too many bad people. So, why not sit here and read instead of fret? God will take me home when it's my time."

"Good point."

"There's nothing we can do but see how it all plays out."

"Hey." Billy grabbed her arm and yanked her from the chair. "Get back over there where I can see you."

"I'm only talking." She jerked free and strode back to where Dani stood, anger replacing fear. Ms. Mayfield was right. Why worry? There was nothing they could do.

The diner's phone rang. Billy ordered her to answer.

Her hand trembled as she lifted the receiver to her

ear. "Hello?"

"This is Sheriff Westbrook. Who is this?"

"Delaney Cooper."

"Is Deputy Hudson in there? Is he okay?"

"Yes to both. Do you want to talk to him?" She took a step in that direction.

Billy shook his head.

"Uh, I'm not allowed to take the phone to him."

"Tell me where the hostages are."

"Lined up in front of the windows but not the door." She lowered her voice and met Billy's curious stare. "They're getting suspicious, Sheriff. Maybe you should talk to one of them."

"Ask him what he wants."

"The sheriff wants to know what you want." She held out the phone.

"Tell him we only want a safe ride out of here. If he doesn't back off, we start shooting people."

"Did you hear him?" She asked the sheriff.

"I heard him. Tell him I'll call back in a few minutes."

Billy and Steve whispered among themselves. The few words she could make out turned her blood to ice. When she relayed the message to the sheriff, he told her to stand back by Dani.

"I have a bad feeling about this," Delly whispered to her sister.

"Yeah?"

"I think they're going to use us as shields if they leave. There's no way the sheriff will let them get into their truck without arresting them."

~

Joey listened to Delly's side of the phone

conversation and tried to fill in the blanks as to what the sheriff had planned. He doubted it would be much longer before either the sheriff or one of the two men made a move.

"You ever been in this type of situation before?" Gary, the chef, asked.

"Once, but the hostages were the man's wife and kids."

"Everyone make it out okay?"

"No. The man shot his wife. She survived, and I shot him. He didn't. The kid made it out fine." Joey prayed he didn't have a repeat of that situation.

The phone rang again, and Delly answered. After a couple of seconds, she set the receiver down. "The sheriff said the way outside will be clear in five minutes." Eyes wide, she glanced at Joey.

The fear in her eyes made him want to jump to his feet and go to her rescue. She knew something he didn't. His hand itched to grab Gary's gun. "Lean against the table," he whispered.

The big man did as he said.

Joey slipped the gun from his waistband and placed it in his lap. "When I say move, I want you to drop to the floor."

He would only have a split second to act when Billy made his move. He couldn't have anyone in the way. Taking a deep breath, he rolled his head to relieve some tension, then using Gary as a shield, he rose to his feet.

Billy aimed his gun at Delly's head and ordered her to leave the store in front of him. Steve pulled Dani close against his chest.

"Move." Joey drew his gun. Gary and Lucy

dropped to the floor at the sight of the gun. Using the distraction, Joey aimed and squeezed the trigger. Billy fell.

Steve shoved Dani away and raised his weapon.

Joey fired again, taking the man down.

Screams rang out as the diner hostages rushed to the front doors.

Tears poured down Delly's face as she ran into Joey's arms.

"I need to check them, sweetheart." He put his hands on her shoulders. "I'll take you home soon, okay?"

She nodded. "I'm being a baby, I know."

"Not at all. Lots of people cry under stressful situations."

She smiled through her tears. "Thanks."

As he felt for a pulse in Billy's neck, the sheriff and Deputy O'Connor rushed inside, guns drawn. "This one is dead."

O'Connor checked Steve. "This one, too."

"Any of the hostages harmed?" The sheriff glanced around the diner.

"No."

He clapped Joey on the shoulder. "Good job. Now, go home. You can fill out your report tomorrow. The twins look about ready to drop."

"They aren't the only ones. It's been one of those days. Since these two are the men who shot at us in Texarkana, I'm guessing the police there didn't find anything."

"Nope. At least they won't be bothering the women anymore." The sheriff shook his head.

"It's going to get worse." Joey straightened.

"Oscar Roberto is coming himself."

"You know this how?"

"I overheard these two talking. He's coming to collect the debt that Dani isn't able to pay." He glanced to where Dani had joined Delly in the booth. "She needs twenty-nine thousand dollars in a week."

"Guess we'd better be prepared. Things will get very ugly very fast."

# Chapter Nine

Uh-oh. Delly set her coffee on the counter and opened the door to the camper when a familiar car door slammed just outside her door.

"Where is she? I'm going to wring her neck." Her mother stormed inside. "Dani?"

Dani bolted upright from the sleeper sofa, her hair tousled. "Gee whiz. Ugh." She fell back and pulled the blankets over her head. "We had a late night, Mom."

"I don't really care what kind of a night you had. You have some explaining to do." She yanked the blankets off. "Delly, coffee."

"In her defense, we did have a rough night." Delly poured two more cups of coffee and set them on the table as she explained about the hostage situation.

Her mother whipped around to face her. "Are you telling me that someone shot at you when you were visiting my apartment, then you were held hostage in a diner?"

"Yes."

She returned her fury on Dani. "This is all your fault. You could've gotten your sister killed. Now, get out of that bed and tell me what you plan to do to rectify this situation."

"For crying out loud." Dani kicked off what was left of her covers and glowered. "Have some sympathy."

"Stop with the teenage theatrics and do as you're told. Oh, you're going to be the death of me."

Delly hoped not. She picked up her discarded coffee and slid into the booth.

Her mother scooted in next to her, leaving the other side for Dani. The interrogation would now begin. Delly was more than happy not to be the one sitting across the table.

"Can I drink my coffee before you start shooting questions at me?" Dani stirred a liberal amount of sugar into her mug.

"No, you cannot." Mom folded her hands on the table and speared her with a sharp look. She didn't say a word; she didn't have to.

Dani started squirming. Even Delly's palms started to sweat around her mug.

"I need twenty-nine—no, make that thirty-thousand dollars by the end of the week. Simply put, I lost too much money gambling and borrowed from a loan shark. I didn't make any payments for over a year, and now he's coming to collect." Her shoulders sagged. "Feels good not to keep that secret anymore."

Mom still didn't speak. Instead, she released a heavy sigh.

"Uh, can you…lend me the money?" Dani widened her eyes. "Mom?"

"Give it to you, you mean. We all know you don't have the means to pay me back." She shook her head. "I'm not rich, Danica. Yes, your father had a nice life insurance policy, but that's supposed to help me live comfortably for the rest of my life. Not be squandered on gambling debts."

"I have a little saved." Delly put her hand on her mother's arm. "I can help."

"Absolutely not." Mom slid from the booth and glared down at Dani. "I'll give you the money on one condition."

"Anything."

"You check into a rehabilitation clinic. Today."

"But what about Roberto?"

"I'll handle Roberto. The difficult part will be withdrawing that amount of money in a week's time." She paced the small space. "I suppose we should also talk to the authorities and see whether we have an alternative."

"Delly is close with one of the deputies." Dani looked hopeful.

"Well, we're working together, or we *were* working together to find Dani." She wasn't sure what more Joey could do. "Where are you staying, Mom?"

"Here. You can share the sleeper sofa with your sister. Dani, go get my things out of the car. All I have are the type of clothes you wear on a cruise. I'll also need to go shopping. This place is bitter cold this time of the year." Mom stormed into the bedroom.

"I'm so mad at you." Delly opened the camper door. "Go get her things."

"Aren't you going to help me?"

"No." Once her sister stepped outside, the temptation to lock her out raised its head. Instead, she opened the door when Dani lugged the suitcases to the camper.

Delly had found her sister. Now, she'd lost the

bedroom to their mother. Well, she wouldn't sleep with her sister on the sofa. She'd choose one of the recliners over sharing with a bed hog like Dani.

"How do you think Mom will handle Roberto?" Dani dropped the bags and shook her arms. "What does she have in those? Bricks?"

"I guess she'll handle him the same way she does us. With a sharp tongue." Delly carried their cups to the sink.

"That won't work." Dani shook her head. "Maybe I should reconsider becoming his mistress."

"Lord, spare me from my foolish daughter." Mom grabbed a bag. "Have I taught you no morals at all?"

"I forgot how good her hearing is." Dani flopped onto the sofa bed. "We're all doomed."

"Probably." Her mother wasn't the only one who wanted to throttle Dani. Delly's world had been turned upside down. She'd been shot at, held hostage, and now lived in a camper. "The two of you have fun. I have to go to work."

"You're working?" Her mother glared from the bedroom doorway. "How are we going to get out of this if we aren't all working together?"

"I need to make money, Mom." Delly grabbed her coat. "Why don't the two of you come by for breakfast? Dani knows the way." She rushed to her truck and fled the campground as fast as she could.

Mom might think she could talk Roberto out of harming Dani, but Delly wasn't so sure. It couldn't be that easy. The man was coming to Misty Hollow. She contemplated leaving, but go where? She had a feeling the man would find them no matter where they went. He probably expected Dani to pay with more than money for losing two of his men.

Possibly her life.

~

Joey glanced up from the booth he sat in as Delly entered the diner. He started to wave but stopped at the look of worry on her face. Something had happened since last night.

She glanced his way, then headed into the kitchen, coming out a few minutes later with her apron on and a coffeepot in her hand. "Need a refill?"

"Sure. You okay?"

"My mother is here."

"Ah. Enough said."

"I'm pretty sure she'll be here soon. You might want to run."

He laughed. "I can handle your mother."

"Sure, you can." She gave a weak smile and moved to the next customer.

What did Mrs. Cooper have planned now that her daughter had been found? Would the three women be leaving Misty Hollow? He didn't have to wait very long to get answers. Dani and her mother arrived at the diner shortly after Delly.

With a glance around the room, then a whisper from Dani, the two headed his way and joined him without an invitation.

"Deputy Hudson."

"Mrs. Cooper." He grinned.

"I don't see the humor in the situation, sir." She frowned. "I have a few questions. One. Where is the closest rehabilitation clinic?"

"There's one here in Misty Hollow and another in Langley." He glanced at Dani who shrugged.

"She'll pay my debt if I check myself in."

He nodded. "Next question?"

"It's not exactly a question." She folded her hands on top of the table. "I need to speak to Mr. Roberto when he arrives in town. Until that time, I need the sheriff's office to help me come up with a plan to convince him not to harm my daughter and/or not have her pay more than the initial loan, which I will pay for her."

He scratched his chin. "You want to meet with a loan shark?"

She nodded.

"And you want to convince him to change his mind?"

"What about this conversation is confusing to you, Deputy?" Her gaze hardened. "Perhaps you aren't the man for the job. I should probably speak with the sheriff, but since you've been helping Delanie, I assumed you could continue in the same way with me. I was obviously mistaken."

"You are not mistaken, ma'am." Delly was right. Handling her mother wasn't easy. "You do know how dangerous meeting with Oscar Roberto will be?"

"Of course. I'm not an idiot. I'm a mother who will do what needs doing to protect her daughters, even if one of them is a pain in my rear end on a regular basis."

"Mom!" Dani crossed her arms, her face reddening. "Stop treating me like a child."

"Then stop acting like one. Why can't you be more responsible like your sister?"

Joey cleared his throat in an attempt to stop a fight. "I'll run this idea by the sheriff."

"You can't stop me even if the sheriff says no."

She hitched her chin. "I can do this myself, but realize how much safer it would be with the backup of the sheriff's department."

"Mother, please lower your voice." Delly stopped at their table and set coffee cups in front of her mother and sister. "You're attracting unwanted attention. It won't take long for the news to spread of what you plan to do." She handed them both a menu. "I'll be back in a minute. Sorry, Joey. She can be a lot to bear."

He raised his eyebrows at Mrs. Cooper. "Anything else?"

"Yes." She handed him her cell phone. "Please put your number in my contact list and the name of the clinic in my map app." She opened her menu, fully expecting him to do as she ordered.

He shook his head but did as he was told. "There you go."

"Have you decided, Mom?" Delly approached and held her order pad.

"Biscuits and gravy for me. Dani?"

"Scrambled eggs and bacon."

"Coming right up. Joey?"

"The breakfast special."

"That's a lot of food, young man. There's nothing worse than an overweight law-enforcement officer." Mrs. Cooper handed over the menus.

Joey glanced at his stomach. "I manage to work off what I eat, ma'am." Not that it was any of her business.

Delly mouthed "sorry" before returning to the kitchen.

He had a feeling she apologized for her family a lot.

An uncomfortable silence settled on the three of

them. Now that Mrs. Cooper didn't have any more questions, she studied the rest of the diner's customers with a shrewd eye. After several minutes, she turned back to Joey. "Do we know what Mr. Roberto looks like?"

He pulled up a photo on his phone and showed it to her. "The women with him are his wife and daughter."

"The wife is lovely. The daughter...looks hard."

He slid his phone back in his pocket as Delly arrived with their orders. They ate in silence. When they'd finished, Mrs. Cooper slid from the booth, shook his hand, and headed to the cash register.

"Again, I'm so sorry." Delly sat where her family had. "She's a lot, but she means well in a strange, roundabout way."

"What do you think about her wanting to meet with Roberto?" He studied her face.

"Really?"

"Yes. I value your opinion."

She sighed. "I don't think it's going to end well. Someone isn't going to walk away from this, Joey."

That's what he was afraid of.

# Chapter Ten

Jessica met Oscar near the Mercedes while her mother, chin quivering, waited on the porch. "Don't sniffle, Mother. This is business."

Oscar, always willing to play the doting husband, gave his wife a kiss on the cheek. "We'll be back before you know. Enjoy the peace, my dear."

"I don't understand why I can't go. Why must you always leave me behind?"

"This is your place, Stephanie. The home would fold if you weren't here. Since our daughter will take over my exporting business someday, it's imperative she learn the ropes." He patted her face a bit roughly, leaving a hint of red on her skin. "I'll call you once we are settled."

"I'm not sure what kind of house I was able to rent for us," Jessica said as she crossed her long legs in the car. "It isn't a very large town, but the house is just over two-thousand-square-feet. That's not much bigger than a cottage."

Oscar patted her knee. "It'll be fine. I don't expect to be there for long." No, he'd swoop in, collect his money and pound of flesh, then be back to his wife within a few days. "The men can sleep on the floor if necessary." He didn't like his daughter being the only female in a houseful of hired thugs, but it couldn't be helped. If they did, they'd find out the consequences of touching her.

He knocked on the window separating the backseat from the front. "We're ready. Coordinates have been sent to your phone. Once we land, you'll know exactly where to take us."

"Yes, Mr. Roberto." The glass lifted, giving them privacy once again.

An hour later, they boarded his private jet and settled in. He opened his laptop to work while Jessica reclined and slept.

His gaze landed on her face. Why couldn't she be beautiful like her mother? Instead, she'd adopted his large features, bulbous nose, overly full lips, thick eyebrows. The only thing she didn't have was his tendency to carry too many pounds on his frame. He wasn't a fool. Oscar knew Stephanie had married him because her father had told her to. How would he find a man to marry his daughter? He sighed and returned his attention to his work.

Several hours later, the plane touched down in Little Rock. They still had a few hours' drive ahead of them. Why did people move to the middle of nowhere? He doubted there would be any of the luxuries he and his daughter were used to.

"Who, exactly, are we after?" Jessica clicked her seatbelt into place in the rented luxury car.

"A woman named Danica Cooper who owes me money for gambling debts."

"Why haven't you killed her?"

He narrowed his eyes. "You can't get money out of

a dead person. Remember that. Killing is only used to prove a point."

She shrugged. "Then a member of her family?"

"It might come to that. She has a mother and a twin sister." Oscar would get his money one way or the other. He hadn't failed yet, and no gorgeous blonde would change anything. He shot his daughter a harsh glance. "Do not take matters into your own hands. You are here to learn and observe, nothing more. Understand?"

"Understood." She crossed her arms, and a scowl covered her face.

By the time they started up the mountain, the beauty of the landscape almost made him forget the inconvenience of having to retrieve the loan himself. Maybe he and Jessica could make a short vacation out of the trip. It had been many years since he'd held a fishing pole.

The house his daughter had rented was a two-story, red-brick house on a couple of manicured acres. A large barn, bigger than the house, sat off a ways. His men could sleep there. He hadn't expected to see something this nice in the country. "How did you find this placee?"

"It's an Air B&B. An expensive one. Seems some people like to spend time in the country." She shoved her door open and stepped out without waiting for the driver to open her door. "When do the others arrive?"

"Sometime this evening." They'd had to fly on a public airline. Unless someone had worked for him for a long time, and he trusted them, they didn't travel on his private jet.

"How are you going to find this Danica?" Hands

on hips, she stared at the house. "Not too bad. You did bring a chef, right?"

"Yes, dear." He rolled his eyes. His daughter was spoiled, and he had no one to blame but himself. "Try to enjoy yourself. It isn't often you get the chance to experience nature."

"We vacation in the Hamptons all the time."

"Not the same thing." He strode toward the house leaving the driver to bring in their bags. "Since the chef isn't here yet, find us a place to eat."

She typed into her phone. "There's only a diner here. I don't think they'll have anything we'd like."

"Call and make a reservation." He pushed open the front door to the house and stepped into a surprisingly stylish room. Yes, they would be comfortable enough here.

"They don't take reservations." She frowned. "What kind of place doesn't take reservations?"

"Simple places. Change into something less flashy so we blend in." He headed up the stairs in search of the master suite.

An hour later, their driver pulled into the parking lot of an old-fashioned diner. "You sure, Mr. Roberto?"

"We'll be fine, Thomas." With Jessica at his side, he entered the diner and followed a slip of a girl to a booth.

Jessica's lip curled. "How quaint. Looks like something from 1950."

"Hush. Don't make a scene. We do not want people to—" His eyes narrowed at the sight of one of the waitresses. Danica. Wait, no...something was off. Her sister perhaps?

~

71

Delly handed the new arrivals each a menu. "Welcome to Lucy's. What can I bring you to drink?"

"A cosmopolitan." The woman opened the menu using only the tips of her fingers as if touching it would give her a disease.

"I'm sorry. This is a dry county. We don't serve alcohol."

"What?" Her eyes widened under heavy brows.

"We'll both have coffee and water…with lemon." The man didn't look up from his menu.

Delly kept a pleasant smile on her face until she entered the kitchen. "We have some newcomers to town. Not very friendly, either."

Lucy peered out the pass-through window. "Yep. I don't recognize them. They have a 'big city' look about them. Wonder what brought them to Misty Hollow? Oh, look, cowboys."

Delly followed the other woman's gaze as five handsome men in boots and cowboy hats took seats at a table. "I don't recall seeing them before."

"I heard there's a new ranch outside of town. The son of a rancher who died took over the place and plans on raising horses and cattle. The girls are going to go crazy over those guys."

Let them. Delly had enough on her mind without a handful of handsome men in hats. She placed coffee and water on a tray and carried it out to her unfriendly customers. "Do you need a few more minutes, or have you decided?"

"I'll have the chef salad." The woman sighed. "Ranch dressing on the side. I can't wait for our chef to arrive."

Chef? Delly tried to keep the surprise off her face

as she turned to the man. "Sir?"

"I'll take the stew. Does that come with bread?"

"Yes, sir. You'll enjoy it. I guarantee it, or the meal is on me." She flashed a smile and went to place the order.

When she returned to the dining room, Joey strolled in. He smiled when he spotted her and headed her way. "Hey."

"Hey." She grabbed a menu. "Want to see this, or do you want the special? It's steak tonight."

"You had me at steak." He slid into his usual booth which happened to be between the newcomers and the kitchen. "Place is busy tonight."

"A lot of new faces. Is this normal for winter?"

"Not really. Spring through fall is when most visitors come. I know why those men are here. You'd better get used to seeing them."

"That's what Lucy said. I'll place your order."

Her mother and Dani entered the restaurant. Dani paled, stumbling when her mother gave her a gentle shove.

Delly followed her sister's startled glance to the newcomers.

The man's narrow-eyed gaze told her all she needed to know. Oscar Roberto had arrived in Misty Hollow.

Joey must have noticed too, because he immediately stood to greet her family.

Delly followed in time to hear her sister tell him that the man was Oscar Roberto, and the woman was his daughter, Jessica. She pulled her sister close. "Get a grip, Dani. You're attracting attention. We don't want a repeat of the other night."

"They're here for me." Her eyes filled with tears.

"Go sit with the deputy. No one will bother you if you're sitting with him. Right, Deputy Hudson?"

"Most likely." He shot a glance toward the Robertos, then escorted her family to the booth.

Delly swallowed past the boulder that had lodged in her throat and went to retrieve the Robertos' food. She pasted on a smile as she set the plates in front of them. "Enjoy. Remember, if you aren't happy with the food, there's no charge, although our chef is a former five-star chef. He fell in love with the town and a woman, and he stayed." Realizing she was rambling, she whirled and headed to the table of cowboys.

Although the men flirted a bit, some of the fear hanging over her dissipated. Roberto didn't seem as if he'd planned on making a move that night. Probably because of Joey's presence. All they had to do was keep Joey around. As if the man didn't have a job. She shook her head and returned to the kitchen.

"What's wrong?"

"Remember the men wanting Dani to pay up the other night?"

"How could I forget?" Lucy shuddered.

"The man she's owes the money to is at table eight."

"Oh." Her eyebrows rose to her hairline. "Chef, do you have your gun?"

"Always. What's up?"

Delly repeated what she'd just said. "I don't think anything will happen tonight. More likely the man is here to shake up my sister." *Oh Lord, please don't have my mother decide tonight is the night to confront him.* Just in case, she rushed back to Joey's table. "Please behave, Mom. Don't start anything."

"Why would I do that? The man is simply enjoying a bowl of stew. It wouldn't be wise to interrupt his meal." She snapped open her menu, showing she was finished with the conversation.

Joey chuckled and shook his head. "Wait to bring my plate when you bring theirs. I don't want to eat in front of anyone."

"Are you off duty?" Mom asked.

"No, ma'am. Just on break."

"Then eat. Dani and I aren't on a time frame."

He shook his head at Delly.

She nodded and went to let Chef Hoover know to wait on cooking the steak. "Table five all want the steak special. Do we have enough?"

"Sure do." He pulled more steaks from the commercial-size fridge. "We're usually packed on steak night. I'm prepared. You holler if I'm needed out there, okay?"

"Will do." Although Mom did seem to be behaving herself. Even Dani was uncharacteristically quiet. Maybe the night would pass without incident.

It took both her and Lucy to carry all the steaks to table five. The men did some more flirting, bringing another smile to her face—a smile that disappeared the instant she turned around.

Oscar Roberto stood beside table seven, the table where her family and Joey sat.

# Chapter Eleven

Joey slid his hand under the table for easy access to his gun. "Can we help you?"

"I've heard this lady wants to talk to me." He shifted his gaze from Joey to Mrs. Cooper and smiled. "Since I'm the only man eating stew within earshot of this booth, it's a safe guess you're talking about me."

"I am, but it can wait." Mrs. Cooper put a pleasant expression on her face. "This isn't exactly the place to make a deal."

"May I?" He nodded to the bench Joey occupied.

Joey frowned and scooted over.

"Jessica, bring my stew, please." Roberto folded his hands on the table and waited for his daughter to bring his meal. "You may return to the other booth."

The woman's face darkened, but she did as she was told.

"Please tell me how I may assist you, Mrs. Cooper." He spooned stew into his mouth.

"At least there is no need for introductions."

Delly stood at the table, worry creasing her forehead. She glanced from Roberto to her mother. "Is this necessary?"

"We're merely talking, dear." Mrs. Cooper hitched

her chin. "Aren't we, sir?"

"Of course." He glanced up at Delly. "Remarkable how much your beautiful daughters look alike."

"They look like their father."

"I beg to differ." He cast a warm glance on Mrs. Cooper.

"Flattery will not work with me, sir."

Joey fought back a grin. This man had no idea who he was dealing with.

She waved for Delly to get their food, then waited, her eyes never leaving the loan shark. Only when her and Dani's food arrived did she start to speak. Joey gave the man credit. He didn't squirm under her scrutiny.

"I have a proposition for you, Mr. Roberto."

"I'm listening."

"Danica will be entering rehabilitation for her...problem in the morning. She'll be there for a month. I can give you the original twenty-thousand, but I ask that you wave the other ten since she is seeking help and the funds are needed there."

He set his spoon down and dabbed at his mouth with a napkin. "What kind of businessman would I be if I waived the interest?"

The tension around the table increased. Joey shifted and put his hand on his weapon.

"One with a heart." Her gaze switched to Joey. "Relax, Deputy, we're merely talking."

Joey couldn't relax. Not after the other night. While it didn't appear that Roberto had brought anyone with him but his daughter, he wouldn't take any chances. Especially when it came to the safety of the three Cooper women.

"There is no more money, Mr. Roberto. You can't squeeze blood from a turnip, so they say."

He laughed. "But you can squeeze blood from flesh. I've given Danica plenty of time to pay up. If I let her slide, people will think I'm soft." He tossed his napkin on the table and slid from the booth. "I will give you thirty days to come up with the full thirty thousand. If you do not, well…We will speak again when night falls on the thirtieth night from tonight." His gaze flicked to Joey. Rather than finish his sentence, he motioned to his daughter to follow him, tossed a hundred-dollar bill on the table, and left the diner.

"That didn't work." Dani folded her arms on the table and rested her head there.

"It bought us more time. That was my intention." She removed thirty dollars from her purse and dropped it on the table near Roberto's bill. "Dani will have a nice tip tonight. Good night, Deputy. We've an early morning ahead of us."

Joey shook his head as they left. With little trouble at all, the woman had managed to buy them a month's time. He didn't know if she'd be able to procure the money, but if anyone could, Mrs. Cooper would be the one. Adding his money to the growing pile on the table, he exited the booth. "You okay?" He stopped where Delly was rolling utensils in napkins.

"That was weird, wasn't it? Or am I really lost?"

"From what I know about Oscar Roberto, that was very weird." The man had allegations a mile long but nothing that stuck legally. He somehow coerced others to do his dirty work, hired good lawyers, and always walked free. "But your mother is a remarkable woman. It's also good that your sister is seeking professional help."

"It is, if she stays. In the past she's checked in and left before she should." Delly put the rolled utensils into a basket. "I'm off work. See you tomorrow."

"Wait." He probably shouldn't, but he wasn't exactly working a case. More like watching to prevent something from happening. "Want to have dinner with me on your next day off?"

"Are you asking me on a date?" A smile graced her lips.

"Yes, I believe I am."

"My mother will have a field day with this, but yes. I'd love to have dinner with you on Sunday evening." She pushed the front door open and stepped into the night.

Joey followed and watched as she drove away. Several dark SUVs drove past the diner. He rushed to his car and pulled out after them. If these were Roberto's men as he suspected, they would lead him to where the man was staying.

They led him outside of town to a large red-brick house whose owners were on an extended trip to Europe. He'd heard they'd rented the place but hadn't thought the renter would be Roberto. Now that he knew where the man stayed, he'd pass the news on to the sheriff and keep an eye on the place.

If Roberto put one toe out of place, Joey would be there to apprehend him.

~

Other than a swarm of men the day after her mother's conversation with Roberto, the rest of the week passed without incident. Dani stayed at the clinic, Mom found a women's group in the local church and signed up to volunteer, and now Delly stood in front of a full-length mirror wishing she'd brought better clothes with her.

She really hoped black skinny jeans and a nice sweater would be dressy enough for her date with Joey. She applied some makeup and left her hair down. A spritz of perfume, and she was as good as she was going to get.

"Lovely." Mom smiled when she stepped out of the bedroom. "I'm glad you're having fun through all this."

"Well, we have a month in which we don't have to worry about Dani." She had no idea how her mother was going to come up with the rest of the money, but whenever she broached the subject, Mom's expression clearly said, 'back off.'.

A knock on the door almost stopped her heart. It had been so long since she'd been on a date. Romance hadn't been on her mind since…forever. Work and her sister had occupied all of her time. *Please, Dani, stay in the clinic for the whole thirty days*. Both Delly and their mother needed the break.

Mom opened the door and invited Joey in. One look at his jeans and a sweater that brought out the green in his eyes put Delly at ease. She wasn't underdressed. Grabbing her coat, she said, "I'm ready."

"Great. How do you feel about Italian?"

"Love it." She smiled. "We must be going to Langley."

"We are." He let her go out before him. "I didn't think you wanted to eat at Lucy's, and she's pretty much the only place in town."

"You thought right." She settled into the passenger

seat of his truck and lost her ability to speak. What was wrong with her? He was the same Joey as the one she knew before he asked her on a date. She cut him a sideways glance. Chiseled features...a manly man despite being called Joey. Handsome, definitely not a "pretty" boy. "Why Joey?"

He chuckled. "I grew up in Misty Hollow. Went to college in Fayetteville, played some football, went to the police academy, and through it all, it's always been Joey. It doesn't bother me. I'm used to it."

"No one ever calls you Joseph or Joe?" She tilted her head.

"They wouldn't dare." His grin widened. "I probably wouldn't answer anyway."

They settled into silence again. She'd never been good at small talk. With a sigh, she glanced out the window and watched as men milled around a large red barn beside a brick house of the same color. "Is that where Roberto is staying?"

"Yep."

"Do you think he'll sit back and wait for the month to end before doing anything?"

"We can only hope. Since Dani is safely in the clinic, the man has no reason to think she'll vanish. He won't make a move until she's out and doesn't get paid."

"Mom will find a way. She has the money, but it's all she has, or so she says. Dad left her comfortable when he passed." Delly kept her gaze on the property until they'd driven too far for her to see.

"Your mother shouldn't have to pay for your sister's choices."

"She has all of our lives." Delly sighed and shifted

in her seat. "Dad traveled a lot, leaving Mom to raise us. When he was home, Dani acted like the perfect child. So, Dad thought Mom exaggerated about my sister's behavior. It didn't help that we sometimes pretended to be each other. Then, 'Delly' got in trouble."

He glanced sideways. "You didn't mention you."

She shrugged. "He loved me, but Dani monopolized his attention. They had a bond I never did. When he died, she went wild. Boys, drinking, then gambling as an adult."

He glanced in the rearview mirror for what had to be the fifth time since they'd passed Roberto's place.

"What's wrong?" She glanced behind them. Headlights pierced the dark, but the car stayed a safe distance back.

"That vehicle has been following us for the last few miles."

"Are you sure?" Her heart leaped into her throat. "What happened to him not making a move? I mean, it has to be Roberto's men, right?"

"There's no law against traveling in the same direction. Let's see what happens when we pull up to the restaurant."

Delly kept watch out the back window until they pulled into the parking lot of Antonio's in Langley. The vehicle, a black SUV, drove past. Her heart rate returned to normal. It made sense Roberto didn't trust her. She didn't trust him either.

Joey held the restaurant door open for her to enter. His constant searching of the parking lot put her nerves on edge again. How could she enjoy her supper if he suspected trouble?

"Can you at least pretend to relax?" She asked as the hostess seated them and handed them menus.

"I'm sorry. It's sometimes difficult to leave the deputy at work when I'm off duty." He smiled, but his gaze flicked to the entrance.

"You think they're going to come here?" She narrowed her eyes over her menu.

"No."

She arched a brow.

"Okay, yes. I think the game he'll play for a month is one of intimidation."

"I might be a scaredy-cat in intense situations, but I don't intimidate easily." Once she moved past the initial fright anyway.

He chuckled. "No, I can see that. You handled the shooting and the diner very well."

"Thank you." She grinned and chose shrimp scampi. Joey did the same along with a glass of wine for each of them.

"Are your parents still around?" She reached for her water.

"No. Mom died of cancer when I was a teen, Dad of a heart attack two years ago." Sadness crossed his features. "I'm an only child. The sheriff's department is my family now. Which reminds me, I need to let Sheriff Westbrook know where Roberto is staying."

"For the next while, he's here it seems." She motioned her head toward the door.

Roberto and Jessica were seated at a nearby table. The man smiled their way before studying the menu.

"I heard them say they had a chef." Delly lowered her voice. "So, why are they here?"

"To make sure we don't know or say anything that

would incriminate them."

"Everyone knows who he is and what he does."

Joey nodded. "Yes, but no one has been able to convict him."

"You intend to try." Fear rippled through her at the danger he took upon himself.

"Yes."

# Chapter Twelve

Early Monday morning, Dani reached for the knob on her room door. It opened easily without a squeak to give her away. She peered up and down the hall. Not seeing anyone, she grabbed the small suitcase her mother had loaned her and stepped out of her room.

Taking a deep breath, she waited. When no cry of alarm rang out, she rushed toward the exit. Although she was free to leave whenever she wanted, she still felt the need for secrecy. If someone saw her, they'd try to stop her, and she couldn't endure another day of lectures and group support.

She'd receive enough lectures from her mother and sister. Still, that was better than listening to a dozen other people's sob stories. People who had far worse addictions than she did. In less than a week, she'd learned what she needed to do in order to stop gambling. There were plenty of apps to "pretend" gamble. She'd satisfy her thirst that way.

A cold blast of early morning air slapped her in the face when she stepped outside. Without a backward glance, she sprinted for the interstate in hopes of hitching a ride. Man, it was cold. She pulled the collar of her jacket higher on her neck and stuck out her thumb as headlights pierced the dusk.

The SUV slowed, then stopped. The passenger-side window rolled down.

Dani stared into the barrel of a gun.

"Get in." The hard-eyed man shoved the door open. "Roberto wants to see you."

She climbed in, her eyes never leaving the gun. "How did he know?"

"That you flew the coop?" The man shrugged. "He didn't. You're just unlucky enough for me to find you hitching a ride. Buckle up. The rest of the day is going to be a doozy."

Dani sighed. Sometimes she had to be the unluckiest person in the country. Today was one of those days.

The man drove her to the rental house after calling ahead to let Roberto know they were coming.

Roberto waited on the front porch, his features set in stone. "Bring her to my office. Don't wake the rest of the household." He turned and strode into the house.

Dani followed without saying a word and stood in front of his desk. Bookcases lined the two walls. A large window overlooked the back property. "Nice place."

"Have a seat." He motioned to one of the leather chairs. "Yes, it is nice. Jessica did well. I thought we'd be here longer, though."

"What do you mean?" She twisted her hands together.

"There's no need to wait a month now that you've decided to leave the clinic. I'll take my money now." He grinned and steepled his fingers. "You've cut my vacation short. My wife will be pleased."

"Please give my mother the month she's asked for. It isn't her fault I can't handle the clinic. I felt claustrophobic."

He leaned his elbows on the top of the desk and speared her a gaze. "It's always something, Danica." He straightened. "I gave you a year. My quandary now is what to do with you if your mother can't pay?"

She swallowed against a desert-dry throat. "Kill me?"

"Killing you doesn't get me my money. All it does is rid the world of a fool."

"Then what are you going to do with me?" She wiped her sweaty palms on the leg of her pants.

"You'll be my guest until your mother pays up. Be aware though, that you are here of your own accord." The tone of his voice said otherwise. "I may have to take drastic measures if it takes too long to get my money."

"What kind of measures?"

"Let's just say you won't enjoy them." He rose to his feet and called in the man who had driven her here. "Take her to a vacant room."

"Want me to lock her in?"

Roberto grinned her way. "No need. She cares about her family too much to run."

Dani knew what kind of measures he would take. Her sister would be the one to pay if their mother didn't come through.

~

"Say that again?" Delly could barely register what the employee of the clinic told her. "Are you sure she's gone?"

"All her things are gone from her room."

"Thank you." She hung up and knocked on the bedroom door. "Dani has left the clinic."

"What?" Her mother yanked open the door.

Delly repeated herself. "If she left before sunlight, she should've made it here by now."

Mom pulled her robe tighter around herself. "Put some coffee on and call Deputy Hudson. My gut tells me Mr. Roberto has her. We'll need to pay him a visit."

"He's going to want his money immediately." Delly's heart raced.

"Yes, but it will take me a while to get my hands on that much. I don't have it in the bank. Instead I'll use the insurance money from the damage to my condo. I'll find another way to do the repairs. Maybe I'll make Dani do them." She closed the door.

Delly wanted to strangle her sister for putting their mother through this. Mom shouldn't have to give up so much because of Dani's poor choices. She planted her palms on the counter and stared out the small window above the sink. If Mom didn't pay, Dani or one of them would die. They had no other option. Turning, she studied the camper. How much could she get for it? Fifteen, maybe? It would take some of the burden off her mother. They could find a house to rent until they returned home. It might work.

With a plan in her mind, she made the coffee and set two cups on the table as her mother, now fully dressed, joined her. "Did you call the deputy?"

"Not yet. I want to run something by you first." Delly sat. "Hear me out before you say no."

Her mother's eyes widened. "I'm not going to like this."

Delly took a deep breath. "I'm going to sell the

camper."

Her mother scowled. "No, you're not. Your father loved this camper. We have a lot of memories in this camper."

"It will pay for half of what Dani owes, so you don't have to shoulder the whole thing." She refused to be swayed. "Father left the camper to me. It's mine to do with what I want, and since he isn't here, I plan on selling it."

"He left it to you to live in until you could get on your feet. You've accomplished that." Mom's eyes flashed. "I appreciate you wanting to help, but I'm fine. In fact, I plan on selling the condo as is. I can live with you girls until I find a place of my own. That way, I don't have to dig into what your father left me."

"You wouldn't have to do any of that if I sold the camper." Delly could be stubborn too. "Mom, things could get very bad if we don't come up with the money and fast. Now that Dani has left the clinic, I doubt Roberto will give us a month."

"He'll have to. I can't sell anything in less than that, and a month is still pushing it close." She rose to her feet without drinking any of her coffee. "The subject is closed. You let me handle Mr. Roberto. Now I need to paint my face so I look as good as possible when we pay him a visit. I suggest you put on something nice."

Shaking her head, Delly watched her mother return to the bedroom. With the camper sold, which probably wouldn't take as long as the condo, they might be able to hold the man off for a bit by giving him half. Delly stood and reached into a high cupboard over the sofa and pulled down a metal, fireproof box that contained important papers. She pulled out the deed to the camper and slipped it into her purse. After dressing quickly, she grabbed her purse and coat and dashed for her truck. Mom would be angry, but she'd get over it once she saw the logic of what Delly was doing.

They needed money fast. Roberto didn't strike her as the type of man to be negotiated with. Not for long, anyway. Thanks to her sister, time was running out.

She drove to a local dealership who offered her thirteen thousand. Refusing to take anything lower than fifteen, Delly started to leave. The dealer said he'd pay fifteen. With the promise to bring the camper within the week, she then went to a local realtor in search of a rental home.

Sight unseen, she signed a six-month lease, praying it wouldn't take that long to get things settled. Then, she headed to the sheriff's office to speak to Joey.

Doris waved her back and reached for the ringing phone on her desk.

Delly stopped in front of his desk. "Do you have a minute?"

"Sure." He turned from his computer and smiled. "I always have a minute for you."

Her face heated as she sat across from him. "Dani left the clinic this morning. She hasn't returned home, so Mom and I think she might be with Roberto."

He frowned. "Oh no. I'll let the sheriff know, and we'll pay the man a visit. Anything else?"

She told him about selling the camper and renting a house. "Mom is furious, but I don't see any other way. I'm hoping this buys us some time."

"Hopefully." He reached for her hand. "You're

doing the right thing under the circumstances. What I'm hoping for is to find something on Roberto that puts him away for a very long time, and you don't have to pay anything."

"That would be awesome." But not realistic since no one had locked him up after so many years.

"Want me to follow you home and speak to your mother? The last thing we need is for her to go see the man."

"If you don't mind." If nothing else, he'd be a buffer against her explosive anger once she heard the news.

Joey pushed to his feet and walked her to her truck. "See you there."

Delly nodded and climbed into the driver's seat. As she drove toward the campground, she steeled herself for against mother's reaction. She stopped at the campground host's cabin long enough to tell him they'd be gone by the end of the week, then parked at her site.

Delly expected her Mom to be waiting at the door, but she wasn't. Neither was she at the table or on the sofa. She rushed to the bedroom. Not there or the bathroom.

She turned as Joey entered. "Mom is gone. Wanna guess where she went?"

# Chapter Thirteen

Roberto glanced out the window as a car he didn't recognize pulled into the drive. He couldn't believe his eyes when Mrs. Cooper emerged from the back seat. She leaned in the window, said something to the driver, then marched toward the house.

One of his men stepped out to block her path. The man had guts holding his ground despite the woman's wagging finger in his face.

With a sigh, Roberto stood and joined her outside. "Mrs. Cooper, to what do I owe the pleasure?"

"Is there somewhere we can speak in private?" She tilted her head. "Or are you afraid to be alone with me?"

A laugh escaped him. "Please, come in." He gave a mock bow, then led her to his office.

"Father?" Jessica glanced up as they passed through the living room.

"Everything is fine." Roberto closed the door to the office and invited Mrs. Cooper to sit. He took a seat in his chair and waited for her to state her business.

"Where is my daughter?" She crossed her arms.

"As of half an hour ago, she's sleeping."

"I'm here to take her home."

He shrugged. "You may do that if she wants to go with you, which I doubt." He folded his hands on the desktop and leaned forward. "You see, Danica is quite content here. In fact, we'll be headed back to New York soon."

She frowned. "What about the money?"

"Do you have all of it?"

"Not yet. You said we could have a month. You said when night falls in a month." Her eyes broke contact with his.

"Your daughter leaving the clinic changed that, Mrs. Cooper." He leaned against the back of his chair. "Night has fallen. The time to pay is now."

"Or?"

He smiled. "Only time will tell." He thought for a minute. "I will stay in Misty Hollow for the promised month, but I will not wait that long for my money. If I don't receive it soon, someone will pay, Mrs. Cooper."

"The other daughter and deputy is here, Father." Jessica stood in the doorway.

He sighed. "Send them in."

~

Delly's heart thumped in her throat at the thought of entering Roberto's house. But...since her mother and sister were both most likely inside, she didn't have a choice. Two things kept her from turning around and running back to the truck: her family's presence inside and Joey's presence by her side.

"It'll be fine. He won't try anything with me here." Joey put his hand on the small of her back.

Roberto didn't seem the type of man who would let a badge stop him from doing what he wanted. Neither did his men, who led them into an office where her mother sat. Roberto's daughter followed them inside, then closed the door before taking a position in the corner. When her father shot her a look, she hitched her chin and met his gaze with a stony one.

"Please have the chef prepare coffee and sandwiches," Roberto said to a man standing off to one side. "It appears we have an impromptu party."

"He refuses to stick to his part of the bargain about giving us a month to come up with the money." Her mother frowned.

"That's fine. I will have fifteen of the thirty thousand to you by tomorrow, Mr. Roberto."

"That's good. What about the rest?"

"It will take my mother a little longer to liquidate some assets." She willed her legs not to tremble under his intense stare.

"Tell me you did not sell the fifth wheel." Her mother shot to her feet and whipped around to face her.

"I have a buyer. Tomorrow, we move into a rental house." She turned back to Roberto. "I'd like to take my sister with us."

He shrugged. "That's up to her. Unfortunately, she had a late night and is still sleeping."

"Wake her up." Delly squared her shoulders.

"It is rude to make demands in someone else's home." His gaze hardened. "Your sister will wake up when she is ready. I suggest you complete your business of securing my funds until she gets in touch with you. Here is my phone number and my daughter's. Give us a call when you have the money, and we'll retrieve it. Until then our meeting is adjourned. Jessica, please see our guests out."

"What about the sandwiches?" Mom clutched her

purse.

"I've changed my mind." One corner of his mouth quirked. "Just as I did about waiting a month. Good day, Mrs. Cooper."

"Let's go."

His daughter opened the door.

Delly glanced at Joey, who nodded.

"Deputy?" Roberto called out. "I suggest you keep these ladies under control. My men and my daughter are exceedingly protective of my interests."

"Is that a threat, sir?" Joey didn't turn around.

"Not at all." Roberto's chuckle followed them out the door.

As soon as they stepped onto the front porch, Jessica slammed the door after them.

"I cannot believe you went against my wishes and sold the camper." Mom's eyes narrowed. "Where is my ride?"

"I sent him away." Joey motioned to his truck. "I'll take the two of you home."

"I do not want to be in the same vehicle with my traitorous daughter." Her face darkened.

"Mom, please." Delly rolled her eyes. "It's the only way to keep Dani safe and not leave you penniless. We'll be fine. Neither of us has used the camper in years."

"But I might have wanted to in the future."

"Then, I'll save and buy you a new one that has all modern features." She stepped aside so Joey could open the passenger side door, then climbed into the small backseat, leaving the front for her mother.

She could handle it if her mother gave her the silent treatment for a bit. Bringing Dani safely home was more important than ruffled feelings.

"Do you think Dani is okay?" She met Joey's gaze in the rearview mirror. "Why wouldn't he let us see her?"

"I'll find out later when I return with the sheriff." He turned the key in the ignition. "I'll do my best to make sure nothing happens to Dani. I promise."

"I know you will." If anyone could help them through this, it would be Joey.

"Anyone up for a late breakfast?" He glanced through the mirror again.

"That would be lovely." Mom kept her gaze straight ahead.

Delly sighed. "Sure." Maybe Mom's cold shoulder would thaw a bit over a good meal.

They hadn't been seated a full five minutes when two of Roberto's men entered the diner. They sent a glance to the booth where she and the other two sat then chose a nearby table. "Guess they're still monitoring our conversation." She flipped open her menu.

"So, we don't talk about your sister or money unless in a private place." Joey glanced at the whiteboard with the day's special. "I want the pancakes."

Delly chose a ham-and-cheese omelet, while her mother ordered chocolate gravy and biscuits. "I've always wanted to try them," she said. "What better day than when I'm worried sick about my daughter?"

"No judgement here." Delly snuck a peek at the two men in creased jeans and ironed button-up shirts. Roberto must insist on some sort of dress code. His daughter dressed in stylish clothes, and she hadn't seen him in anything but a suit.

One of them caught her eye and gave her a grin that sent ants trickling down her spine. Shark eyes. Dead eyes that held no emotion whatsoever. She shuddered and turned away.

~

Sheriff Westbrook listened without speaking until Joey finished telling him about Danica Cooper being with Roberto. When Joey stopped, he rubbed both hands down his face. "Let's go have a talk with the man. I don't want him causing trouble in my town. Especially with all the suspected crimes the man has committed in the past."

Murder, fraud, kidnapping...Joey had read his file. "I want to find something on him that sticks. If we find out that Dani is being held against her will, we'll have it."

"That's a mighty big if." The sheriff stood and ambled out the door. "Doris, hold my calls. I'll pick up my messages this afternoon."

"You got it, Sheriff."

Once in the sheriff's car, he asked, "You sure Roberto has put a tail on Delly and her mother?"

"Yep. At least two men show up wherever she is." He told him of his theory about not talking about what was going on with Dani. "Obviously, the man thinks she knows something or has the money—something that makes him want to keep tabs on what she talks about or where she goes."

"Unless she's being held against her will, there isn't much we can do. Keep an eye on her and her family as often as you can."

That went without saying. Not that he was complaining. He enjoyed spending time with Delly, and he'd seen her every day since her arrival in Misty Hollow. "I'm going to check out her rental house tomorrow. Make sure it hasn't been bugged. Even though she just rented it, I doubt Roberto misses much."

"Good idea." The sheriff pulled into Roberto's driveway. "I've always liked this house. From now on, though, I won't be able to look at it the same way. Since this woman doesn't know me, I'll let you question her."

For the second time that day, Joey approached the front door. He couldn't help but wonder how long his luck would hold before his goons met him with violence. How long would Roberto's polite demeanor last?

He hadn't missed the look of disdain his daughter bestowed on them when he'd arrived with Delly. Who would cause the most trouble, the daughter or the father? Did he want to know?

"Again, Deputy?" Jessica Roberto opened the front door. "With reinforcements, even. Pardon me if I don't invite you in."

"We would like to speak to your father." The sheriff removed his hat. "It's fine if we speak to him out here."

Her cold smile told them they didn't have a choice. She closed the door.

By now, several men had gathered on the well-manicured lawn. All big, all muscled, all with stern expressions. Nothing more than hired goons who did Roberto's bidding.

More than twenty minutes later, Roberto joined them. "Sorry to keep you waiting, gentlemen. I was on a business call. Please, have a seat." He lowered onto a rocking chair. "Would you like something to drink? Water, coffee, or tea? I know how much you Southerners like your sweet tea."

"Nothing, thanks." The sheriff exhaled heavily. "Is Danica Cooper here?"

"Yes." Roberto smiled.

"May we speak to her?"

He snapped his fingers for one of the men watching. "See whether Danica wants to speak with these men."

The man rushed past them and into the house.

"So, she's awake now." Joey didn't bother removing his hat. The man didn't deserve but the barest of manners.

"Of course. It's afternoon." Roberto shook his head. "You act as if we're keeping her prisoner."

"Are you?" The sheriff asked.

"Ask her yourself."

Dani stepped out of the house. "Sheriff. Deputy." Wary eyes flicked from one to the other. "You want to speak to me?"

It didn't look as if they'd have any privacy. Joey nodded. "Your mother and sister were here earlier."

"Really?" Her hand fluttered around her neck. "I slept in."

"Are you here of your own free will, Dani?"

Her gaze shifted to the left. "Yes. I'm...uh...working off some of my debt?"

She lied the same way as her sister. By answering a question with a question. "Why did you leave the clinic?"

"I didn't like it there. Boring people, boring

meetings…I can handle this on my own."

"Really?" He arched a brow. "Do you have the money to pay this man?"

"Not yet."

"Do you realize your sister sold the camper in order to pay half your debt? That she has now rented a house here in town?"

She paled. "She loved that camper."

"Obviously, she loves you more. Why not leave this house and go to her? Your family is doing a lot to make sure you're safe."

Her eyes veered toward Roberto but she stopped and shook her head instead. "Since I don't have a vehicle, it's easier to stay here. I'm the…maid?"

Another lie. He wanted to laugh but kept his "cop" face in place. "It will take you a long time to work off thirty-thousand dollars."

"I know." Her shoulders sagged. "But, with my family helping, it won't be as long as you think."

He exchanged a look with the sheriff. "If you need me, you know where to find me."

"I'm good here." This time she did look at Roberto who gave her a nod. "Thank you for your concern." She rushed back into the house as if the hounds of hell chased her.

Maybe they did. Joey headed back to the car, the sheriff at his side. Once in the car, he said, "She's lying."

"How do you know?"

"Because both she and Delly answer with a question mark at the end of their sentence when they lie. She isn't here voluntarily."

# Chapter Fourteen

With a check for fifteen-thousand dollars in her purse, Delly inserted the key into the lock of the rental front door. "It isn't much, but it's home for now. Best part is…it comes fully furnished, even if it's stuck in the eighties."

Joey waved his arm for her to enter first. "Two-bedroom, two bath will suit you and your mother fine."

"Don't forget my sister." She scowled. "I intend to get her away from that man. So, what exactly are we looking for?"

"Listening devices, tiny cameras—anything that will allow Roberto to keep tabs on you."

The thought chilled her blood. "Thank you for doing this before we move in this afternoon." Everything they had with them now sat in boxes in the back of her truck waiting to be unloaded.

Still angry, Mom waited at the diner, most likely complaining to anyone who would listen. When she tired of that, she'd visit the bank to start the proceedings of withdrawing a large sum of money from her savings.

At least, Delly hoped that's where her mother was and not off bothering Roberto. Once they were finished checking out the house, she'd deliver the check to the man in hopes of convincing him to hold off making Dani pay in some other way.

Delly sat on the hideous orange and brown sofa depicting a hunting scene while Joey searched every nook and cranny of the small house. Maybe she could find some seat covers to improve the look of the furniture. Her mother would have a coronary as soon as she walked in the door.

Joey plucked a small silver disc from under a lampshade and dropped it on the heavy wooden coffee table. "That's one."

So, it was true. Roberto had discovered which house she'd rented and bugged it. Delly slouched against the back of the sofa. She was no match for a man like him. Thank God, she had Joey as a friend and protector.

She watched as he continued to search the room. Once again, he'd given up a day off to help her. Clad in faded jeans and a flannel shirt that matched his eyes, he made some serious eye candy. His heart was as beautiful as his exterior. Why hadn't some lucky woman snatched him up?

Regret over the fact she didn't have the freedom to pursue a romantic relationship swept over her. If she did have the time, it would be with him…if he wanted.

"I found three listening devices in every room, plus a recorder. Even in the bathroom." He set them all on the table. "This man knows no boundaries."

"What do we do now?"

"I'm fairly certain the house is clean, but I'm going to have someone else do a sweep anyway. Just to make sure I didn't miss anything." He sat next to her. "When we're finished, you'll be safe here."

"I should install an alarm system." Another expense she really couldn't afford.

"If I ask, I'm sure the landlord will install one." He smiled. "He can charge higher rent next time. Let me give him a call. What's next on your agenda today?"

"Nothing?" Her voice squeaked.

"Delly…"

"Fine. I'm taking the check to Roberto." She waited for him to say he'd come with her and—.

"Not alone, you aren't." He swept the electronic bugs into the palm of his hand, then into his pocket. "I also need to take these to the sheriff's department. We don't have solid proof Roberto put them there, but it's one more suspicion to hang over him. I won't stop until this man is behind bars."

She put a hand on his arm. "Please don't do anything dangerous. He'll slip up at some point. They always do, right?"

"He hasn't so far." He put his hand over hers. "Ready?"

"Let me check on my mother." She pulled up a tracking device on her phone. Her mother was at the bank. "How long do you think it will take for her to withdraw the amount she needs?"

"If she doesn't need to wait on the insurance company, a couple of days. Either way, you two should be able to pay off Roberto within the week."

Delly really hoped so. She'd like to go home. Or did she? Texarkana held nothing for her anymore. No job, just a house she didn't really like. Not even her mother had a place anymore. Why not stay in Misty Hollow after everything was said and done and see what the future held?

She'd had worse ideas.

"Want to ride with me? There's no sense in both of us driving, but I do want to stop at the office." Joey stopped near his truck as rain fell from the sky.

"Sure." Delly liked spending time with him, even if it was to stop a madman. She threw him a smile over the hood, then slid into the passenger's seat. No reason for him to come around and open the door for her and get wet. Not on a cold winter day.

Inside, he cranked up the heater. "Let's hope Roberto is open to receiving only half of the money. Either way, don't let on we found the bugs, okay? Let him think he's pulling one over on us."

She nodded. "I'll do whatever you say."

"Sure, you will." He laughed and backed his truck from the driveway. "You might pretend to do what I say, but you, Miss Delaney, will do exactly what you want."

Yes, and that fact often got her in trouble.

~

Joey was becoming a regular visitor at Roberto's. Again, his passage was blocked as he and Delly headed to the porch. Again, Roberto stepped out and told the men to let them pass.

"What can I do for you this time, Deputy Hudson?" Roberto crossed his arms. His daughter copied him, looking every bit the female version of himself, minus the middle-aged paunch.

Delly moved forward and held out the check. "Half of what my sister owes you. I'd like to take her home now."

His daughter snatched the check from her hand.

"Not until the full amount is paid, Miss Connor." Roberto smiled. "Thank you for the check. Anything else?"

She glanced at Joey, then back to the man. "You should have the rest by the end of the week."

"Very good." His grin widened. "It's a pleasure doing business with such responsible people. You should teach your sister."

"Let her come with me, and I will."

"Good day, Miss Connor."

"May we at least see Dani?" Joey noted the twitch of a curtain in the front window. "To relieve some of her sister's worry?"

"I think not. In this case, worry is a good thing, Deputy." He returned to the house.

His daughter shot them a look of amusement before following. Something about her set Joey's nerves on edge. What was she up to, and did her father know? If the daughter was trying to make a name for herself, she might be more dangerous than Roberto. Someone needed to keep an eye on her. He was starting to feel stretched way too thin. "Come on." With his hand on her lower back, he guided Delly back to the truck.

"I really wish I could've at least seen her." She buckled herself in. "How do I know she's okay?"

"Unless we know she isn't safe, we must believe she is." He gave her hand a squeeze. "He can't retrieve his money without Dani."

"That's true." She sighed. "I just want this all to be over."

"Hang in there." He drove them to the office. "This won't take long. Then, we can meet your mother for lunch at the diner if you want to contact her."

"I'll send her a text." She waited in the reception room while he headed for the sheriff's office.

Sheriff Westbrook stared at the electronic bugs Joey set on his desk. "All of these? That's a bit of overkill, isn't it? Maybe the guy wanted them to be found. Wanted Delaney Cooper to know no lock could keep him away."

The thought hadn't occurred to Joey, and it sent chills down his spine. "You think the danger could be escalating? So far, he's been more of a minor harassment."

"If he doesn't get his money soon, yes. Hopefully, it will happen this week as you believe. Otherwise, we don't have enough manpower to stop him and his men. They'll go through this town like a swarm of locusts."

"Let's pray that doesn't happen. There's something else. I think the daughter might be worse than the father. The evil behind those dark eyes of hers makes me want to hide under the blankets."

The sheriff stared at Joey. "Well, I always said a man should trust his instincts. What's your plan?"

"It's hard to keep an eye on the woman if she never leaves the house. Sir, not that I care much for Roberto, but Dani isn't the only one in danger in that house."

"I'll have deputies make regular visits to the house. As long as Roberto himself comes out, we'll know he's fine. You keep watching the Cooper women, but also try to dig something up on the man that will put him away for a long time."

Joey nodded, then escorted Delly back to the truck, then to the diner where her mother had already chosen the same booth Joey always sat in. Except, she sat on his side. "Would you please trade places with me?"

"Why?" She narrowed her eyes. "That side is the same as this side."

"I prefer not to have my back to the door."

"Mom, switch places." Delly took ahold of her mother's elbow. "What is wrong with you?"

"I don't see why it makes a difference."

"If I'm facing the door, I can see trouble coming before it's too late." He slipped his cop face into place. "I must insist you move to the other side of this booth."

"Fine." She rolled her eyes, ignored Delly, and slid into the other side of the booth.

With a heavy sigh, Delly slid in next to her. "Still not speaking to me, I see. Well, the check is in Roberto's hands. Joey found a lot of bugs in our rental home—not the creepy crawly kind. Our boxes are still in the back of my truck. We need to go home after lunch and unpack."

Her eyes widened at the mention of the bugs, but she kept her attention on the menu in her hand. "Thank you, Deputy, for checking out the house."

"I'm going to have someone else come by this afternoon to do another sweep." He glanced at Delly's mother whose head was buried in the menu.

Delly snorted and shook her head. "If someone keeps acting like this, I'm not going to let her have the master bedroom."

"Ha!" He bit back a laugh. Would *his* mother have been this stubborn if she'd lived to be…what? Fifty-something? Joey didn't have a lot of experience with middle-aged women. He definitely admired Delly's patience.

The bell over the door jingled.

Two of Roberto's men walked in and took the nearest table to the booth where he sat with the two women. Joey met their cold stares with one of his own. It might be his day off, but he still carried a gun in his waistband and wouldn't take any grief or allow anyone to give grief to the two women across from him.

He almost wanted to dare the men to make a move.

# Chapter Fifteen

Jessica carried two cups of coffee into her father's office as she did every morning. Grinning, she handed him his, sat across from him, and crossed her legs. Her gaze never left his face.

"You seem chipper this morning." He slurped his coffee and grimaced. "Needs more sugar."

"Today is the day everything will be as it should be." She could barely contain her excitement. "Here." She tossed him a packet of sugar. "Forgot how much you took in your coffee." What she didn't know was how much sugar his coffee needed to disguise the taste of an additive. She kept a smile on her face as he stirred in the sugar and took another slurp. For such a powerful man, her father really was a pig.

"Better, but the coffee tastes...burnt." He shrugged and handed her a file. "You want to help, read this. I, uh..." His eyes widened as he swayed in his chair. "What did you do?"

"What needed to be done. You've gone soft, my dear Father. Swayed by a pretty face." She rose to her feet and dropped the file back on his desk. "You should've made Danica Cooper pay for reneging on the loan a long time ago." She planted her hands flat on his desk. "Now, it's you that pays the price before I finish her by ridding the world of her twin first."

"But…they're…paying."

"Not fast enough. Your empire is now my empire."

"You won't get away with this."

"Oh, but I will. You see, you boarded a plane this morning. You were seen holding your ticket."

"I fly private."

"Not today." She smiled. "Engine trouble. I've thought of everything."

He groaned. His head fell forward with a thunk on the polished walnut desk.

Jessica exhaled heavily and stepped into the hall to where a man waited. "Ricardo, get rid of the body where no one will find him for a long time. Tell the others who's boss now. Then, fetch me our guest."

Shouldn't she feel some remorse for killing her father? She turned and stared at his lifeless body and shrugged. Remorse, no. She felt nothing but pity for her foolish mother who would mourn his death.

~

Dani slapped a hand over her mouth to stifle a gasp and ducked into the closest room. A bathroom. She closed the door as quietly as possible and turned the lock. There had to be a way out before Ricardo came for her. How long did she have? How long would it take for him to dispose of Roberto? An hour? How would he hide the body?

She covered her face with her hands and lowered to the toilet seat. Her mind whirled with too many questions. She needed to concentrate. Now was not the time to panic.

Deep breaths, Dani. One, two, three…

She had nothing in her room she needed. Standing in the shower, she glanced out the window. Thick woods lay between the house and the railroad tracks. Dani shoved open the window and pulled herself up. It would be a tight fit, but being thin had its advantages. She sucked in as much of her body as she could and shimmied through the window. Her shirt caught. Yanking it free, she fell out, landing in a juniper bush. With the breath knocked out of her and scratches covering every exposed surface of her skin, she struggled to her feet. After a quick glance around, she sprinted for the trees. Once out of sight, she felt for her cell phone to give her mother and sister a heads-up.

Nothing. Dani's gaze locked on the bush she'd fallen into. She must've lost her phone when she fell. There was no way of contacting anyone unless she found a phone. No. She'd head straight to the sheriff's office. Would they believe her about Jessica killing her father? If they paid the woman a visit, they'd see for themselves.

She slapped a low-hanging tree branch away from her face and kept running. A grunt from somewhere to her left stopped her. She peered through some thick foliage to see Ricardo digging a hole. Roberto's body lay nearby. Sticking out of his pocket was a cell phone.

All she needed was a weapon in case Ricardo caught sight of her. She grabbed a stick as thick as her wrist and crept forward, stopping every foot or so. The man kept digging and mumbling under his breath.

Dani slowly reached for the phone. It slipped easily from Roberto's pocket, and she melted back into the trees with the man none the wiser. Things were finally going her way.

A train thundered past. She screamed, then froze. When the man digging Roberto's grave didn't come after her, she raced down the track beside the train knowing it would mask the sound of her flight.

Roberto's rental was at least five miles from the sheriff's office. It would take her all day to make it that far, and after her last hitchhiking ordeal, she didn't trust not getting picked up again by one of Roberto's...Jessica's goons.

She eyed the phone in her hand. Deputy Hudson would come pick her up. She made the call, telling him she'd meet him next to the road, then laid the phone on the railroad track so the next train would destroy any tracking device it might have. Life on the streets had taught her a thing or two.

From her place behind a tree, she kept watch for the deputy's squad car.

~

Joey slowed as he neared the place Dani said she would be. She darted from the trees and toward him, fear etched on his face. When she'd called, all he could make out was that she'd escaped and where she would be.

"Thank God." She climbed in and buckled her seatbelt. "Let's go straight to the sheriff's office. Jessica Roberto killed her father."

"Wait. What?" He jerked to face her.

"I'll tell you everything when we reach the office."

The man couldn't be dead. Joey had followed him to the airport himself on the orders of Sheriff Westbrook. The sheriff wanted the man watched every time he left the house. If Joey hadn't followed Roberto, then who had he followed? "Are you sure?"

"I saw his body." She wrapped her arms around herself as if trying to get warm.

It didn't take long to arrive at the sheriff's office. Joey escorted her straight to the sheriff. "You'll want to hear this." He motioned for Dani to have a seat.

"I'm listening." The sheriff crossed his arms.

Dani explained about hearing Jessica tell a man named Ricardo to get rid of the body, then how she herself had escaped out the bathroom window and then saw Ricardo digging a grave with Roberto's body nearby. "I snuck up, stole the phone, and called you."

"Where is the phone now?"

"Hopefully lying in pieces on the railroad track."

Joey shot a look at the sheriff. "Why?"

"I'm sure Jessica would know I had it once she discovers I'm gone, then pings her father's phone."

"Deputy Hudson followed Oscar Roberto to the airport this morning."

"That couldn't have been him. I saw his dead body! Why don't you believe me?"

Joey put a hand on her shoulder as she started to stand. "It isn't that we don't believe you; it's more like we need to check into this further."

"That woman will hurt my family." She struggled under his hand. "You need to make sure they're safe first."

"I agree." The sheriff nodded. "Hudson, I want you staying at their house with them. Not one single Cooper goes anywhere without you. Preferably, everyone goes as a group. Not that I don't think Jessica Roberto would hesitate to harm the entire family, but she might at least think twice. Security?"

"Alarm installed the other day. I'll pack some

things and take them over when I take Dani." It wouldn't be the first time he'd slept on a sofa. "Sir, the daughter will be far more cold-blooded than the father. It might be time to call in reinforcements."

"If we find out that Oscar really is dead, it'll be no off-duty days for any of us."

Joey nodded and led Dani from the room. After picking up a few things from his place, he drove to the diner.

Delly's eyes widened at the sight of her sister. "How?"

"Is there somewhere we can talk in private?" Joey asked.

"Sure. Lucy will let us use her office." Delly glanced from her sister to him, confusion in her eyes. She led them to an office down a short hall and closed the door. "Tell me."

Dani started, telling her sister everything she'd told Joey, then turned the conversation over to him.

"So, in an attempt to keep the three of you safe, I'll be sleeping on your sofa. None of you goes anywhere unless all four of us go. Where is your mother?"

Delly paled. "Running errands. Groceries, I think."

"I'll make a call and have her picked up. I'm really sorry it's come to this." He wanted to smooth the stricken look from her face.

"Let's just get this over with. One Roberto's down, one more to go." She squared her shoulders. "What else can we do?"

"Nothing right now." He smiled, admiring her spunk. "What time do you get off work?"

"Seven. I'm safe enough here. There's always plenty of people."

He wanted to say no, but she was right. Plus, the chef never went anywhere without his gun. "On one condition."

"Okay."

"You aren't even to take out the garbage. You do not leave the inside of this diner until I arrive to pick you up. Understand?"

Her face darkened. Delly's flashing eyes let him know she didn't like to be ordered around, but then they softened. "I understand."

"Good. I'm going to take Dani home now. When I come for you later, I'll pick up burgers for supper." He smiled. "We'll make it through this, Delly. I won't let anything happen to you or your family."

"You'll do your best." A knock at Lucy's office door pulled her attention away. "I need to get back to work."

Lucy opened the door and peered inside. "Oh, I'm sorry, Joey. I didn't know you were here."

"We've just finished. Lucy, I'm asking for your help in making sure Delly does not go outside for any reason. I'll bring her to work and pick her up."

"I'll make sure she doesn't. All it would take is a few words to the diners, and everyone will be looking out for her."

Delly shook her head. "I don't want anyone involved that isn't absolutely necessary. The danger is too great." She strode out of the room.

"I don't think she likes your plan much." Lucy grinned. "What about you, Dani?"

"Looks like I'll be a prisoner in my own home."

It took all of Joey's strength not to mention how this was all her fault. If she'd made better choices, no one would be in danger of losing their life. But, she wasn't the first addict he'd come across. Empathy worked better than berating them. "Let's see if we can't get ahold of your mother."

Since he hadn't heard from Deputy Matchett, worry trickled through him. Bridgeton had one grocery store. It shouldn't be that difficult to locate Mrs. Cooper. Unless, she'd gone somewhere she hadn't mentioned to Delly.

He led Dani to his car and placed the call to Matchett.

# Chapter Sixteen

Delly glanced up as her sister and Joey reentered the diner. The look on Dani's face told her they had more trouble.

"You'll need to come with me." Joey glanced at Lucy, then back at Delly. "We need to find your mother."

Her heart dropped. "What do you mean?"

"I sent a deputy to find her, and the deputy told me all the squad cars except mine had slashed tires."

"In the sheriff's parking lot?"

"Apparently. Let's go."

"I have to tell Lucy." She rushed to her boss. "I'm sorry to leave you short-handed, but—"

"Go. I'll call in someone to fill in for you. Never put your job before family, Delly."

"Thank you." Delly gave the woman a quick hug, then darted to the supply room for her purse and coat before following Joey and Dani to his car. She slid into the front passenger seat. "Mom said she was going grocery shopping."

"And she might be. Either way, we need to reach her before anyone else does." A muscle ticked in his jaw.

117

Dellyt glanced at her sister who remained uncharacteristically quiet. Seeing that she looked miles away, Delly would leave her be for a bit. Maybe some heavy thinking would open her eyes to what she'd caused. Why did some people have to learn the hard way while dragging others along with them?

Her sister met her gaze with the saddest eyes.

Delly's heart melted, and she smiled. "Mom will be fine. She's the strongest woman I've ever met."

Dani sighed. "I know." She returned her attention to the window.

Joey pulled in front of the grocery store. "Stay close. No one gets separated."

"She left an hour ago. Her car is still here." Delly stepped inside the store. "Do you think she's—?" Why hadn't her mother answered her phone? Delly had texted her the instant Joey and Dani had first left the diner to let her know Dani had escaped.

A blast of warm air greeted them inside the store. As it was still mid-morning, not a lot of shoppers wandered the aisles. It shouldn't be difficult to find her mother.

They glanced down each aisle as they traversed the store. No sign of her. Joey questioned a cashier who said she remembered their mother coming in, but she didn't see her go out.

"Anywhere she might be?"

"I suppose she could be in the manager's office, but she didn't seem to have any complaints."

Delly frowned. "Where's the office?"

"Through the swinging double doors in the back of the store. You'll see a door with a sign that says Manager."

Delly shot Joey a worried glance and headed in that direction.

"Hold up. Let me go first." He stepped in front of her.

While she appreciated his desire to spare her from something she might not want to see, this was her mother. She rushed ahead and pushed the double doors open.

A giggle came from down the hall. A man laughed.

Delly peeked around the corner. Her mother and a man around her age conversed next to a stack of crates full of vegetables. Occasionally, her mother would giggle again. *Giggle?* Something she didn't remember ever hearing.

"Mom?" She stepped into sight.

"Oh hello, dear. This is Rick Simpson, the store manager." High spots of color dotted her cheeks. Was her mother blushing? "Oh, Dani's back."

"Yeah." Delly narrowed her eyes. "We really need to talk to you, Mom. I texted you."

"I didn't hear my phone." She gave Rick an apologetic smile. "Call me."

"Guaranteed," the manager said.

Her mother gave the man her number? Delly shook her head.

"I'll explain everything at the house," Joey said. "One of the deputies will bring your car."

"This sounds serious."

"It is." He strode from the store, leaving the women to follow.

Even though Mom asked several times, no one told her why they'd come for her. Not until they were back at the rental, and Joey had seated her at the kitchen table did he tell her anything. Joey hadn't known her long, but he knew how to handle their mother. In order to make her listen, he needed to be "bigger" and in control.

"Are you going to tell me what this is about?" Mom crossed her arms. "Did Roberto release Dani because Delly gave him the check?"

"Roberto is allegedly dead." Joey stood in front of her. "We still have to confirm that, but Dani swears she saw his body."

"I did! I used his phone to call you."

"That is confirmed."

While she knew Joey was a deputy, Delly hadn't ever seen him so serious before. The man was scared, which frightened her more than she already was.

"Dani overheard Jessica Roberto tell one of her men to hide the body. She escaped out the bathroom window. The sheriff and I believe the daughter to be more dangerous than her father. So—" He dropped his overnight bag on the floor. "I'll be sleeping on your sofa until this is over."

Mom glanced from him to Dani to Delly and back to Joey. "All right. We brought plenty of blankets." She glanced around the house. "I don't know what else we have, but I'm sure it'll be sufficient."

"Aren't you worried at all about what Joey just said?" Delly's frown deepened.

"Of course, I am, but we can't change a thing, can we? Not without a plan."

"No plan." Joey shook his head. "Let the authorities handle this. We aren't dealing with nice people."

"Of course."

Uh-oh. Mom had an idea cooking in her brain. Delly needed to distract her. "So, what's this about Rick Simpson and you giggling like a teenage girl?"

Her mother smiled. "I was looking for...darn it. I left my cart of groceries."

"I'll have a deputy pick them up when they bring your car." Joey carried his bag to the living room.

Mom planted her elbows on the table and speared Delly with a sharp look. "Now that he's gone, we need to come up with a way of trapping Jessica Roberto. Dani is the bait."

~

Jessica stared at Ricardo. "You're sure his phone wasn't on his body when you buried him?"

"Positive. I checked his pockets." He tossed her father's wallet on the desk.

"Hmm." Jessica had tried to call the phone to see whether it rang inside the house, but the phone must have been shut off. She shrugged. "It's time to create some chaos. I don't care who you choose—a vagrant, maybe—but we need to keep the sheriff's department so busy they don't have time to bother with me. Let me focus on the Cooper women. I want bodies dropping like flies."

"Yes, Boss." He left her office.

Jessica folded her arms behind her head and propped her feet on what was now her desk. This country life was quite enjoyable, and she had no desire to return to New York. Misty Hollow would become her empire. All she had to do was beat the sheriff and his deputies into submission, and the town would be all hers.

Killing her father had gained her the respect of his

men. *Her* men. The strongest lion takes over the pride. Isn't that how the animal kingdom worked? She grinned. It had been so easy, her father so trusting.

It hadn't been difficult for her to bring his coffee every morning. Then, a bit of poison, and voilà! She was now the boss. Things were going to get fun.

~

Joey had just settled on the sofa later that evening when his phone rang. "Hudson."

"The Cooper women all right?" Sheriff Westbrook asked.

"Asleep in their beds." He sat up. "What's wrong?"

"It might not be related, but we discovered a body near the homeless community by the lake."

"Do you want me to check it out?" He reached for his clothes.

"No, you're needed there. I just wanted you to be aware."

"This isn't the first dead, homeless person, Sheriff."

He sighed. "It's the way the man was killed. Execution style, then his fingertips cut off and his teeth removed. Sounds like a mob hit, and there's only one mob in town."

"It doesn't make sense, sir. What would JR have against a homeless man?"

"I didn't say it was a man."

"Wow."

"It's a young blonde, around the same age as the twins."

Joey's mouth dried up. "Ah, an example."

"That's what I'm thinking. Be vigilant, Deputy.

Things are heating up. I'm calling for reinforcements first thing in the morning."

"Keep me informed." Joey hung up and set his phone on the coffee table. For the first time in his career, he felt inadequate for the task. JR, as he'd started calling Jessica Roberto, was an anomaly. They didn't know much about her. The unfamiliar had replaced the familiar and made her more dangerous. Instinct told him to take the Cooper women and run. His head told him that they'd never agree.

"What's wrong?" A tousle-haired Delly emerged from the hall. "I heard talking."

"The sheriff called to inform me about a dead woman by the lake." Since he didn't want to worry her, he kept the information to a minimum.

"Roberto?"

"Maybe." He forced a smile. "It's okay. Might not have anything to do with Jessica at all. Go back to bed."

"I can't sleep. Care for some company?"

"I'd love some." He scooted over.

Instead of sitting at one end of the sofa, she sat close to him and nestled her head on his shoulder. A gesture that felt as normal as the sunrise every morning. He rested his arm along the back of the sofa, his fingers brushing her shoulder.

"She's going to come for us, isn't she?" Delly's question rose barely above a whisper.

"Most likely." An icy fist clenched his heart.

"People are going to die."

"Yep." His voice grew husky at the looming terror he couldn't stop.

"I'm glad you're here with us."

"Me too, Delaney, me too." He closed his eyes and

prayed for strength to power through the F5 twister about to hit Misty Hollow.

He held her until she fell asleep, then laid her on the sofa and covered her up with one of the blankets Mrs. Cooper had left out for him. Taking the other blanket, he moved to the recliner, doubtful he'd get much sleep. Despite the thoughts that had swirled through his mind, he did fall asleep and woke to soft voices and the aroma of bacon coming from the kitchen. He glanced at the folded blanket on the sofa, not surprised to see Delly had woken up.

The hushed conversation raised his suspicion. He quietly slipped from the chair and padded barefoot to stand outside the kitchen.

"I don't like the fact you're going to send me out there alone," Dani said.

"We aren't. Your sister and I will keep you in our sight at all times. When someone comes to grab you, we'll turn the tables on them and demand they take us to see Jessica. Don't worry. I have your father's handgun."

Joey's heart fell to his feet. They planned on holding JR at gunpoint and do what?

"They could have me shot sniper style," Dani's voice rose.

"Shhh. Jessica won't do that. She wants you to suffer as an example to anyone who doesn't take her serious."

"I'm liking this less and less the more you talk, Mom." Delly's hushed voice joined the other two.

"You told me yourself that Joey agrees more people will die unless this ends. We're trying to prevent that from happening. It's our civic duty."

The woman was stark raving mad. She was going to get them all killed.

Joey entered the room, arms crossed, and glared at the three women. "Absolutely not. I'll lock all three of you up for your own safety if you persist. Since you were not to go anywhere without me, I'm fairly confident your conversation was just a pipe dream."

The stubborn look on Mrs. Cooper's face said he was wrong. If the woman could find a way, she would.

# Chapter Seventeen

Jessica's eyes widened as the door to her office opened. "Mother?" Did she know her husband was dead? How would she react? Why should she be worried? She'd taken down her father and gained an empire.

Her mother's eyes flashed. She set her designer clutch on a side table and sat in a leather chair, crossing her long legs. "So, you did it."

"Did what?"

"Don't play games, darling. You rid the world of your father. What are you hoping to gain from it?" She arched a finely tweezed brow.

"How did you know, and how did you find me?" Jessica crossed her arms. She'd always hated how beautiful her mother was. How weak. Why couldn't she have passed on even a bit of her beauty to her daughter?

"You don't really think me as dumb as your father did, do you?" She tilted her head and gave a sly smile. "I've always known, even before we married what his 'business' consisted of."

"Then why act like a doormat all these years?"

"I had a comfortable life, everything I wanted…except his love, which I found elsewhere."

She studied manicured nails. "And I expect the same lifestyle from you. I'm also demanding a partnership in this business." Her eyes hardened. "I'm the daughter of a crime boss, married to a crime boss, now the mother of one. So, from this moment forward, I will no longer stay in the background."

Who was this woman? Jessica narrowed her eyes. "If I say no?"

Her mother snapped her fingers. Two of the largest men she'd ever seen entered the room and stood behind the chair where her mother sat. "These two will make you regret that."

"You'd harm your own daughter?" She tried to look injured but failed as her features became set in stone.

"Hush, darling. You killed your father. We aren't so different, you and I." She rose to her feet. "I'm going to freshen up. When I return, I want to know why Oscar came to this horrible mountain town, and how we can finish what he started and return home."

"I'm not going home. I'm claiming this town for my own."

"We'll see." Mother's patronizing tone made Jessica want to strangle her. Her mother strolled from the room. "Please show me to the master bedroom."

Jessica's blood boiled. She'd claimed that room as her own. Now, she had to figure out a way to get rid of her mother despite those two massive human bookends.

~

Mom dried a plate and set it in the cupboard. "Look at this way. Several nights have gone by, and we're all still breathing."

Delly stared at her mother, mouth agape for a

second before she snapped it shut. "Is that supposed to be some kind of consolation? We're prisoners in this house."

"Oh, pooh." She lowered her voice and glanced at Joey. "I'm working on that."

"Lord, help us." Delly pulled the stopper out of the drain. "I have to go to work which makes me the lucky one. At least while I'm working, I'm not stuck here."

Joey glanced up from his laptop. "We'll all be taking you to work."

"Yes, I know." She sighed and stared out the kitchen window, wanting it all to end so she could get on with her future. Delly had thought she wanted to explore a relationship with Joey, but his highhandedness lately gave her second thoughts. Could she be with a man who ordered her around? Or would it stop when the Robertos were all locked up or dead?

With a sigh, she headed to the room she shared with Dani to change into her work clothes. Her sister sat cross-legged on the bed, papers spread out in front of her.

"What are you doing?" Delly pulled a pair of black pants from the closet.

"Trying to make sense of Mom's dumb plan. I think she's trying to kill me." She flopped dramatically back on the bed and put an arm across her eyes.

"Wasn't it your idea to be bait?" Delly tugged on her pants and reached for a yellow sweater.

"In a moment of insanity. I've been around the Robertos enough to know that Jessica is a sociopath. She has no conscience. I've seen her order a man beaten because he wouldn't—well, no need to go into the gory details."

"Mom thinks that if they do take you, it will only be until we collect the rest of the money."

Dani sat up. "Then, they'll kill us all. JR won't let us live after we give her the money. She won't let us live much longer if we don't. We're doomed either way, oh twin of mine."

Delly refused to believe it. They'd make it out of this somehow, then she'd make her sister go to rehab if she had to handcuff them together. No more decisions that endangered their lives. No more decisions that took their life savings. "Mom will have her money in another day or two."

"Great. We have a day or two to live."

"Come on. I have to go to work." Shaking her head, Delly joined her mother and Joey back in the kitchen. "Dani is busy feeling sorry for herself. She might need some convincing to get up. I really don't want to be late for work."

Joey's phone buzzed. A blood vein stood out on his forehead as he looked at the screen. "I have to go. I'll drop the three of you off." He glanced at her mother. "Don't get excited. I'll have an entire group of bikers watching over you at the diner. You won't be able to get away from them." He typed into his phone.

She grinned. "I have no idea what you're talking about."

He glanced up at her. "Right. Dani, let's go. Now!"

"What happened?" Delly's breath caught.

"We have another murdered blonde."

~

Dave agreed to have a few of his men watch the Cooper women until Joey could pick them up. Thankfully, several Harleys sat outside the diner when he pulled up. "The leader is named Dave. I guarantee you three will be as safe, if not safer, than if I were here."

"Thank you." Delly shoved her door open. "I'm sorry about the woman."

"Yeah, me too." The second one in a week. He doubted she would be the last. Hopefully, the promised reinforcements would arrive later today. As soon as the diner door closed behind the Cooper women, he turned around and drove toward the homeless community.

Crime-scene tape had been tied around several trees, keeping the news van from coming too close. Head down, Joey rushed to where the sheriff and a handful of officers from Langley stood, ignoring the pleas of the new reporter, Linda Williams, for a statement.

"Good, you're here. Follow me." Sheriff Westbrook led Joey to where a woman lay under the low-hanging branches of a pine tree.

Blood from the slit in her throat soaked the fabric of her forest-green, wool coat. The scarf around her neck might once have been a bright yellow. The beanie on her head had slipped to cover one eye. In her right hand, she held a royal flush.

He jerked his attention back to the sheriff. "This is definitely a warning to the Coopers."

"That's why I wanted you here instead of playing bodyguard. You've good instincts, and I wanted you to see with your own eyes how the danger is escalating."

"How can we protect the homeless community?"

The sheriff sighed. "I'll have to spare manpower to make regular drive-bys. These people won't like it, but it's for their own safety. I'd like you to go around and tell at least the blond women what the danger is. See whether anyone saw anything. I have a hard time believing this woman came this far from the community after dark."

"Someone lured her here?"

"That's what I'm thinking. See if you can find out how. Enlist Dave Wakes or Buster Jones to watch the women during the day. I need you here."

"Sure." Buster, the retired cop, could watch the women at home, follow them around, leaving the biker leader to keep an eye on Delly. "They've all been great help in the past. What about the men you deputized?"

"It might come to that." The sheriff marched away.

Joey bent over the body. The woman looked to be several years older than the Cooper twins, but she did seem to be a natural blonde. He straightened. Several different colored canvas tents of the homeless community dotted the distant landscape. Time to circulate and try to chat with people who had a distrust of law enforcement. He zipped up his coat and set off through the trees to the field.

He stopped at every tent and cardboard box and makeshift shelter spreading the news of the danger. At one, a blond woman in her twenties scowled at him from under a ragged hoodie. "I don't talk to cops."

"I'm here to let you know you could be in danger."

"Like the woman who got killed last night?"

"Yes. We believe someone is targeting blondes from this area." He hunkered down to meet her eye-to-eye. "Can I call a shelter for you? Anywhere would be safer than here."

"Mary was my friend."

"Is that the woman's name who was killed?"

She nodded.

"Did you see or know why she left her tent?"

"No, but she wouldn't have left unless someone offered her money or alcohol. She loved her drink. Too much, really." She raised red-rimmed eyes. "For someone who doesn't talk to cops, I'm rambling on, aren't I?"

"Anything you can tell me might help us catch who killed her."

"Nobody cares about us."

"You're wrong there. I care. The sheriff's department cares, or the sheriff wouldn't allow this community to stay here. What is your name?" It pained him to hear that she thought no one cared.

"Amy."

"Help me to help you, Amy. Let me take you somewhere safe. You and any other blondes here. Can you take me to them?"

She shook her head. "I'm not running from my home. Trust me. I'm not going anywhere with anyone I don't know. There's only one other blond woman here. She's in the red tent with the zebra duct tape. Her name is Carolyn." She disappeared into her tent.

By the time he reached Carolyn's tent, a group of men had gathered in front. One of them, obviously the spokesperson, stepped forward. "We'd like to speak to you, Deputy."

"Sure thing." He forced a grin. "What can I help you with?"

"It's more what we can do to help you. I'm Hank. No need to know my last name. Me and the other guys have been talking about how to protect our women."

"I'm listening." His smile faded. The last thing he

or the sheriff wanted was a vigilante group.

"You know how back in the old western days, the wagons circled when trouble came?"

Joey nodded.

"Well, we figure we'll do that. We'll put all the men's tents and places of residence in a circle, real close, and put the women in the center. Ain't no one going to get to them that way. Plus, we all got sticks and baseball bats. We protect what's ours. What happened to Mary, and Jane the day before, ain't gonna happen again." He crossed his arms and fixed his stare on Joey. The other men did the same. "You'll have to arrest all of us in order to stop us from doing this."

Joey glanced from face to face. They could use all the help they could get, but he couldn't let them break the law. "Okay. But, it's self-defense only. Do not go looking for the killer. Do not jump anyone. You suspect someone, you call me. Got it? Otherwise, it's a no, and I'll have the sheriff come out and tell you so."

Hank turned to his buddies. "Everyone understand that?" Heads nodded. He turned back and thrust out his hand. "It's a deal, Deputy."

Joey shook his hand, then headed back to his car hoping he wasn't making a big mistake.

# Chapter Eighteen

Delly stared out the diner window as two black SUVs sped down the street. They looked exactly like the ones she'd seen on TV crime shows.

"FBI has arrived." Dave shook his bald head. "Takes a few deaths before they show up. Last time, we had a riot in the streets. My gang against another one paid to wreak havoc. We won." He grinned.

"I'm sure you did." She chuckled and refilled his coffee. "Now, that they're here, maybe this will end."

"Or maybe it will get worse."

That thought sent ice through her veins. She passed the booth where her mother and sister pored over sheets of paper, planning the "trap" like a couple of war generals. Delly wanted no part of it. Nothing good could come from using her sister as bait.

The group of cowboys new to town entered the diner, laughing and joking with each other and chose a table large enough for the five of them. They removed their hats and set them on the table.

Delly pasted a smile on her face and headed their way. "Good afternoon, gentlemen. What can I get y'all to drink?"

They ordered coffee.

"I'm Dylan Wyatt, owner of the Rocking W ranch. What's going on in town?"

"Some trouble from a New York crime boss's daughter. The sheriff's department is handling it. No need to trouble yourselves."

He glanced around the table. "What do you guys say about offering our services to the sheriff after lunch?"

Affirmatives all around.

"That's kind of you, but—"

"Ma'am, we're all ex-military. Our services can be useful."

She nodded. Let Sheriff Westbrook handle these men. She turned to head to the kitchen when Jessica Roberto and a beautiful woman in a simple sheath dress and pumps entered the diner. The woman stuck out like a rose among thistles. Every head turned as the hostess led them to a booth.

Despite the woman's loveliness, Delly bet she wasn't going to be a nice addition to town. The hard glint in her eyes belied the serene smile on her lips. Taking a deep breath, Delly went to take their drink order. "Good afternoon, ladies." She forced her voice to sound as pleasant as possible despite the urge to toss hot coffee in Jessica's face. "What can I bring you to drink?"

"Chardonay, please." The woman's smile never dimmed.

"I'm sorry. We don't serve alcoholic beverages."

"Seltzer water?" She arched a brow.

"Mother, this is a small town. Regular water will be fine." Jessica rolled her eyes.

Mother? The two looked nothing alike.

"This is my mother, Stephanie Roberto. She grew weary of waiting for my father to finish his business, so here she is."

"Don't tell everyone our business, darling." Stephanie flipped through the menu. A small frown appeared between her eyes. "This is simple fare."

"Our chef is a five-star chef from New York. I'm positive you'll be pleased. Let me bring your waters." She couldn't reach the kitchen fast enough.

"Chef, we have a lady wanting fancy food."

Chef Hoover turned from the grill and grinned. "I can make anything look fancy. Take her order and let me do the rest."

"It's Roberto's widow." Delly poured two glasses of ice water and added lemon. "I'm not sure she knows her husband is dead."

"She'll find out soon enough."

Delly rushed the iced water out, then filled cups of coffee for the cowboys. After taking their orders for steak and eggs, she returned to the Robertos. "May I take your order?"

Stephanie set her menu precisely on the edge of the table. "I don't see it on the menu, but I'd like eggs Benedict."

"I'm sure the chef can do that. Jessica?"

The daughter's thick brows lowered. "What kind of game are you playing, Cooper? I'm still waiting on the rest of my money."

"You'll have it this week." Delly's smile faded as she lowered her voice. "Which means, you can stop killing defenseless homeless people."

"Whatever do you mean? You're mistaken." Jessica smiled with as much kindness as a shark. "I haven't killed anyone."

"Enough." Stephanie Roberto put a hand on her daughter's arm. "Give the server your order."

"I don't know why we couldn't have stayed home. We have a fine chef." Jessica slapped her menu closed. "The bacon Swiss burger and fries."

"She'll have the chef salad." Stephanie's smile chilled.

Maybe Delly had Jessica wrong. While the woman was dangerous, her mother seemed more so. How could it be possible that every Roberto that came to town was worse than the last?

Delly stopped at her mother's table before turning in the order. "Put that stuff away before Jessica and her mother see something that will get you killed."

"The mother is here? I should introduce myself." Mom started to slide from the booth.

"Absolutely not. If you head her way, I'll ask one of Mr. Wakes' men to sit here with you. I'm not kidding. Just leave them alone until the money comes in."

"I told you that won't be the end of things." Dani crossed her arms. "It's best we take them out now."

"Let the sheriff's department handle this," Delly hissed.

"Okay, sweetie." Mom waved a hand in dismissal.

Ugh. Delly stormed to the kitchen and turned in the orders. "Can you make an eggs Benedict?"

"Yep." The chef reached for the eggs. "It'll take a bit since I don't have any hollandaise sauce, but I'm sure she's used to waiting at restaurants." He pulled steaks from the fridge. "Everything will be all right, Delaney. Misty Hollow has seen her type before. Have faith."

Delly tried. She really did.

~

"Welcome, Agents." Joey thrust his hand toward Special Agent Snowe, then Larson. "The sheriff is waiting in the conference room. We've set up a case board." He started to lead them back, then stopped as a group of cowboys entered the building. "Go on back, Agents."

Joey approached the other men. "Can I help you?"

"It's more about us helping you. I'm Dylan Wyatt, and I'd like to speak to the sheriff."

"Wait right here." Joey hurried down the short hall and into the conference room. "Sheriff, before we start in here, some men out front want to speak with you."

"Did they say about what?" He glanced up from a stack of papers.

"Something about helping us."

The sheriff followed Joey back to the waiting men. "I'm Sheriff Westbrook."

"Dylan Wyatt." He offered his hand. "We're all ex-military, special forces, and we'd like to offer our services for whatever is happening in this town."

"We could really use you and your men patrolling the streets if that's doable. Don't want to take away from your work." The sheriff smiled. "But I'd sure appreciate your help."

"What do we do if we find something suspicious?"

"Hold onto it or them and call the office. I don't have the manpower to patrol the streets. We're stretched thin watching over the Cooper women and the homeless community."

"Consider it done." Wyatt left the building, his

men following.

"I wasn't expecting that to happen today." Joey stared after them.

"Me neither, but their help is welcome. Let's fill the agents in on what we know."

Once they returned to the conference room, the sheriff outlined everything that had happened since Oscar Roberto arrived in town.

"The only person who saw the body is this Danica Cooper?" Snowe asked.

"Yes." The sheriff nodded. "Roberto's wife has arrived in town. We aren't aware at this time whether she knows of his daughter killing him or not. In fact, we don't have actual proof the man is deceased."

"But, there's been no sign of him?"

"No."

"No one has been by to ask to see him?"

"He's allegedly in New York on business," Joey spoke up. "Someone used a plane ticket under his name. His private jet is down for repairs. We asked the NYPD to look for him. They'll let us know what they find. So far, nothing."

"We'll have our office there do some searching." Larson stood and pulled his cell phone from his pocket as he stepped out into the hall.

"We don't have anything on the Roberto women that warrants us bringing them in," Snowe said. "Despite the deaths of those homeless women, we don't have the proof we need. We either need an eyewitness or for them to trip themselves up."

Or for the Cooper women to set a trap, something Joey definitely didn't want. Since they were being watched every minute he wasn't with them, he didn't see how they'd manage.

Once the meeting ended, and the agents headed to the only motel in town, Joey set off for the diner to grab supper and pick up the women. Dave Wakes assured him that he hadn't spent his entire day there. The men had taken turns.

"I do hope we don't have to spend every day, all day at the diner." Delly's mother shot him a sharp look.

"No, ma'am. When you aren't here, Buster Jones, a retired police officer, will watch you."

"You're making us prisoners in our own home." She poured a liberal amount of sugar into her tea.

"No, I'm doing my best to protect you."

"You're wasting your time."

"No, he isn't." Dani shook her head. "If I'd stayed at the clinic, things probably would've gone the same."

"We'll never know, will we?" Her mother patted her hand.

"Let's eat so you ladies can go home." Joey wasn't in the mood to hear the same argument he'd been hearing since Marilyn arrived.

At seven p.m., Delly let him know she was ready to go home. Exhaustion coated her pretty face. Joey could relate. Nothing sounded better than kicking off his shoes and stretching out on the sofa. He eyed the papers sticking out of Marilyn's purse and wondered how he could catch a glimpse of them without her knowledge. The woman and her daughter were up to something, and he needed to know what.

Delly caught him looking and shrugged. "I'll tell you later," she mouthed.

Good. That gave him hope that she wasn't a part of whatever crazy scheme the other two were cooking up.

"Lucy gave me some leftover possum pie. Anyone want some?" Delly carried a white box into the house and set it in the center of the table. "It isn't often there's any possum pie left over."

"Sure. I can't turn down my favorite pie. Let me take a quick shower first."

Fifteen minutes later, the four of them sat around the table, finishing off the pie. His gaze fell on Delly. She closed her eyes as her lips settled around the dessert on her fork. He suddenly wanted very much to be that fork. What would it be like to kiss her? A real, long kiss that went to the very core.

Delly's eyes snapped open and caught him looking. Her cheeks flushed.

He yanked his gaze back to the dessert. Now was definitely not the time to pursue romance. Not to mention the fact she kept him at arm's length most of the time because of his ordering the women around. Not one of them liked to be told what to do. Unfortunately, their safety rested on his shoulders.

"Would you help me wash these?" Delly stood and gathered the empty plates.

"Sure." Now he could find out what her mother and sister were up to. He turned on the tap water as hard as it would go. "Tell me."

"It's a simple plan, really. They plan on sending Dani out at dusk alone with the rest of the money in her backpack. Mom will hide in the shadows and record the exchange, only coming out if they try to harm Dani. My mother doesn't think they will, but Dani does."

"And what do you think?"

She took a deep breath, then released it long and slow. "I think it's the dumbest idea I've ever heard, and

Dani is asking to be killed."

Joey thought the same thing.

# Chapter Nineteen

Joey opened the door before dawn the next morning to a serious-faced Buster Jones. "What happened?"

He jerked a thumb over his shoulder. "Homeless community. Sheriff wants you there."

Behind him, an orange glow lit up the early morning sky. "Come in while I get dressed." After one more glance at the burning sky, he grabbed his bag and made a dash to the bathroom.

When he returned, all three of the Cooper women stood watching out the window. Delly turned. "Those poor people."

"I have to go. Buster will take care of you. He'll drop you off at work and bring your mother and sister back here." He grabbed his weapon and badge. Noticing the tears in her eyes, he gathered her close, nestling her head against his chest. "It's going to be okay."

"I'm not worried about me. I'm upset because the Robertos choose those who have so little as their targets." She raised her face to his, making him want to kiss her tears away. "Go, stop them, Joey."

"I will." He smiled and stepped back. "You three

are in good hands with Buster." Although they were in good hands, he hated to leave. But he had a job to do if things were ever going to return to normal. He really wanted to find out what normal with Delly would be like. With one last glance at her, he stepped outside and pulled the door closed after him.

Fifteen minutes later, he skirted fire trucks and stood next to the sheriff. "Anyone hurt?"

"We don't know yet." Sheriff Westbrook peered over Joey's shoulder. "Looks like the fire started at both ends."

"Arson?"

"Looks like it. There's no way to salvage anything."

Joey spotted the men he'd spoken with the day before and headed in their direction. He did a quick head count. "The women?"

"We sent them into the woods," Hank huffed. "We tried to put the fire out, but we couldn't."

"Did you see anyone who didn't belong?"

"Not a soul, but we were all sleeping."

The heat of the flames as the wind kicked up forced them all to step back. Joey eyed the dry winter grass of the meadow. The trees seemed far enough away not to catch fire, but if the flames spread... "We need to keep this from burning the grass." He rushed to the fire captain and expressed his concern. "Those men are willing to help. Do you have shovels?"

"Sure do." He called for someone to fetch them. "A trench might just work if the wind doesn't worsen. Men, lay those hoses on the grass. Tent city can't be saved."

Joey grabbed one of the shovels and headed for the

far end where the meadow sat the closest to a stand of pine trees. Within minutes of digging, sweat poured down his back, and he had to remove his heavy coat.

Two of the men who'd lost their tent pitched in to help until both were overcome with heat and smoke and returned upwind. On occasion Joey had to catch his breath, then cough, his eyes streaming. Even though the fire seemed to be gaining the upper hand, he continued to dig, tossing dirt onto the encroaching flames.

The heat increased. The crackle of the fire drowned out all sound. A strong fit of coughing overcame him, and he stopped and turned around, leaning on the shovel until he caught his breath.

Joey couldn't fight this side alone; he needed reinforcements. He started to turn again when something struck him from behind. The second hit took him to his knees. The third knocked him unconscious.

He came to as Hank and another man dragged him away from the flames. "Dude, you okay?" Hank bent over him.

"Someone hit me."

"Yeah. Someone in a thick coat. They hit you with a baseball bat, then fled into the trees. I think they wanted you to burn to death." He helped Joey to a sitting position. "You were starting to catch fire when we reached you."

"Thanks. You saved my life." Joey struggled to his feet as another fit of coughing bent him over. He wanted to head after his attacker. His lungs and head said otherwise. "Help me to the fire truck, will you?"

The sheriff met them and took over, helping Joey the rest of the way as Hank chattered on about the attack. When the man finished, the sheriff pulled

Deputy Johnson and Young off the fire and sent them to investigate. Both men seemed relieved to have off-fire duty.

"Do you need to go to the hospital?" Sheriff Westbrook peered into his face as a paramedic put an oxygen mask on Joey.

He shook his head and mumbled no. Oxygen and aspirin would be sufficient. Maybe. Hopefully. This was no time to be down.

The paramedic shined a light in his eyes then felt around on his head.

Joey winced and pulled back.

"You have quite the knot on your head, Deputy, and a concussion. You also need a couple of stitches. My advice is for you to take it easy for a few days."

Joey pulled the mask away from his face. "Can't do that. Fix me up and send me on my way."

"You'll have to go to the ER for the stitches. That wound needs to be cleaned."

Joey hopped from the back of the truck and swayed.

"Whoa." The sheriff caught him. "I'll drive."

~

Delly listened as rage rose in her. Someone had attacked Joey as he fought the fire. When the sheriff finished filling her in, she turned to Buster. "I need a ride to the hospital. Joey was attacked."

Her mother gasped. "We'll all go. That poor boy."

Hardly a boy, but she appreciated her mother's reaction. Delly called in to work and left a message that she wouldn't be in that day, then hurried to dress. Joey would need a ride home and for someone to drive his truck. Since Buster needed to watch over her mother

146

and sister, that left the truck and Joey up to her.

The Misty Hollow clinic had what was needed to patch Joey up, and a nurse led Delly to the back as soon as they arrived. The nurse pulled a curtain open. "The doctor will release him in a few minutes."

Delly rushed to the bedside. "How are you feeling?"

Joey took her hand. "Like someone hit me with a baseball bat." He grinned. "Thank you for coming. I didn't know who else to have the sheriff call."

"I'm glad you did." She smiled and wiped some soot from his face with her sleeve. "After all, you're staying with us." There were so many things she wanted to say. How angry and worried and frightened she was, but none of them seemed to fit in that place. Not with Joey lying there injured. He could've been killed. She almost told him she'd decided to go along with her mother's crazy scheme. This had to stop.

"That isn't the only reason I called you."

"I know." She raised his hand to her lips. "You're the one I would've called too."

"Not your mother?" He grinned.

"Heavens, no." She laughed. "They're in the waiting room. Buster will drive them home. We'll follow in your truck."

"Is it outside?"

She nodded. "Someone must've brought it for you. I'll drive. You'll rest."

"I'm capable of driving."

She gave him one of her mother's famous looks that said not to argue with her. Then, she stepped back as the doctor arrived with his release papers.

"Take it easy for a day or two, Deputy. You're

going to have a doozy of a headache. I've prescribed some pain meds if you need them. Come back in a week to have the stitches removed." He handed Joey the papers and left.

"Guess that's it." Joey swung his legs over the bed and slowly stood. "See? I'm able to walk on my own."

"I'm still driving." Delly looped her arm with his and joined the others in the waiting room. "Buster, you'll follow with Mom and Dani?"

"Sure will. Good to see you up, Deputy." Buster held the door open.

By now, the sun had risen, kissing the mountain with shades of rose and pumpkin. Delly remembered that sight from their days camping when their father was alive. Despite the trouble brought on by her sister, she still loved Misty Hollow. She really hoped nothing would change the way she felt.

After another short argument with Joey, she climbed into the driver's seat. "You should recline. It won't take long to drive home."

"Not long enough to try resting, that's for sure."

"You are a very stubborn man." She turned the key in the ignition.

"You are a very stubborn woman." He laughed, then squeezed his eyes shut. "Don't make me laugh."

"I'm not trying to." Still smiling, she backed from the spot and headed toward home. Almost immediately, headlights loomed in her rearview mirror as a vehicle pulled between them and Buster's car, forcing Buster to pull back.

There wasn't a lot more that drove her nuts than a rude driver. She frowned and increased their speed by a couple of miles per hour.

The first hit to their bumper barely made her lurch against her seatbelt. The second snapped her neck.

Joey turned in his seat. "How long have they been back there?"

"Since we left the hospital. Right away, they separated us from the others." She tightened her hands on the steering wheel.

"Can you drive defensively? We're almost home, but don't stop there. Drive on past and head for the sheriff's office."

"I'll do my best to get us there in one piece." Her heart lodged in her throat. Did the driver behind them think she was Dani, or did they no longer care who they threatened or harmed?

Her cell phone rang. Joey grabbed it and put it on speaker. "She's busy."

"There's another one behind us," Buster said. "They're boxing us in. Where we headed?"

"Sheriff's office. I'm calling them now." He hung up and glanced at Delly. "No one better than Buster to lead them there."

She nodded. "Is this where they try to kill us, or is it another scare tactic?"

"Let's hope for the latter."

Another ram and she bit her tongue, tasting blood. She turned and headed down Main Street. Not much farther.

Those who braved the cold morning watched with wide eyes and slack jaws as the line of cars sped past. Delly's hands started to perspire. What if the light turned red? What if someone started to cross the street? She wiped her hands on her pants one-by-one, then quickly regripped the wheel.

"You're doing great." Joey patted her shoulder. "I can see the sheriff's office. Not much farther."

Delly yanked the wheel and turned into the parking lot, stopping inches from the double glass doors. She turned in her seat as Buster did the same and the two vehicles following them raced past, the windows too dark for her to see the drivers. She sagged in her seat. Whew, she'd done it. She'd driven them safely to their destination. "Can we go home now?"

Sheriff Westbrook opened the door and stared at the hood of Joey's truck before his gaze swept the street. His eyes flashed as he motioned for her to back up.

Within seconds, cowboys on horses surrounded the two trucks.

# Chapter Twenty

Delly shifted in her seat to face Joey. "What in the world is going on?"

"The Rocking W Ranch is going to help patrol the streets." He grinned. "I doubt much will make it past these guys."

"Wow. Just like the Wild West." She couldn't drum up the same level of excitement Joey seemed to have. All she could think about was how many more innocent people were taking their lives in their hands.

Sheriff Westbrook tapped on the passenger window and motioned for Joey to lower it. When he did, the sheriff's brow furrowed. "Got another body, and it isn't from the homeless community."

"Who is it?"

"The hostess from Lucy's. We don't know yet whether it's related or not. Do you feel like heading over there and asking some questions?"

Delly started to protest, but Joey stopped her. "Sure, I will." He then glanced at Delly. "I can ask questions while sitting down. This is no time for me to be idle."

She glanced at the sheriff for help. "The doctor said for him to rest."

"I'm sorry. We need him." The sheriff slapped the top of the truck. "Let me know what you find out. I'm going to let these cowboys know what to do." As he said that, the roar of motorcycles filled the streets. "And them, I suppose. Well, I did ask for help. Now, we have more than I need."

"Let's head to Lucy's." Joey closed his eyes and rested his head against the back of the seat. "Don't worry. I'll be fine. This isn't my first concussion."

"It's a good thing I'm not your mother." She backed away from the building.

"Yes, it is." He chuckled. "It would be very, very wrong for me to feel about my mother the way I feel about you."

Delly smiled despite her resolve to be angry. Yes, it would not be a good thing for her to be his mother. She glanced in the rearview mirror to see Buster following them. Good man. He followed without question in case they might need him. She parked as close to the building as she could with two squad cars and an SUV blocking the way. Through the window, she could see diners sitting at tables waiting to be questioned and released. Joey would have to cross the entire parking lot. With a sigh, she shoved her door open. He was out seconds after her, and she linked her arm with his. "Take it slow."

"I'm not an invalid."

"Doctor's orders."

He smiled and tucked her arm closer to him. "I like that you worry about me."

"Hmmph." She returned his smile and opened the door to the diner.

A red-eyed Lucy bustled toward them. "She's in

the alley, Deputy. Next to the dumpster. This is terrible."

"Wait here." Joey slipped his arm free.

"No way. You might need me." She looked back as Buster and the others rushed toward them.

"What is it?" Mom asked.

"Someone killed the hostess, Amber." Delly shuddered.

"This isn't the first-time blondes have been triggered in this town." Buster made a noise deep in his throat.

"That wasn't the same at all. This isn't a serial killer." Joey marched toward the back door with Delly on his heels.

Her stomach rolled before she saw the body. Her breakfast rose to her throat, and she took deep breaths to keep from throwing up.

Amber lay next to the dumpster, a spilled bag of garbage next to her. One of her slip-on shoes lay nearby. Blood pooled under her head.

Joey bent over the body. "She doesn't look like the other girls."

"You think she knew her killer?" She wrapped her coat tighter around her.

"Maybe. I need to question Lucy and the waitress." He straightened and ushered Delly inside. "Until we know more, you stay inside."

"Why don't you sit in your usual booth, and I'll bring you some coffee?" She'd do anything to get him off his feet. "Buster and I can send people your way."

"The other deputies and the FBI are doing most of that. I'm interested in the chef, Lucy, and the other waitress."

"I'll send them over one at a time."

He nodded and slid into a booth.

Delly returned a few minutes later with coffee and Chef Hoover.

~

"Thanks, Delly," Joey said with half a smile.

She nodded and made the rounds with the coffeepot.

"Thank you for speaking with me, Chef." Joey widened his eyes as Marilyn set a notebook in front of him.

"I noticed you don't have anything to write on." She smiled and rejoined Buster, who moved intimately close to her side.

"They look cozy," Hoover said.

"He's only been with them a day." Joey shrugged. "What can you tell me about Amber?" The pain pill the nurse had given him started to wear off. He wanted to do the questioning and return to Delly's so he could at least make her happy by pretending to rest.

"Not much. I stay in the kitchen and don't have many conversations with the female staff." He sat back and crossed his arms, a shadow crossing his eyes. "I was the one headed out with the trash. Since we were busy, as you can see from the full tables, Amber took the bag and said she'd do it so I could keep cooking. She'd be alive if I'd taken out the garbage."

"You don't know that. Did she have a boyfriend? A run-in with a customer?"

"Not that I know of."

"Thank you. Call the office if you think of anything that might help. Could you send Lucy over?"

"Sure thing." He stood and went to where Lucy

dabbed at her eyes with a napkin.

A minute later, she sat across from Joey. "I cannot believe this has happened."

"Do you know of anyone who might have wanted her dead?"

Lucy shook her head. "Amber was a sweet girl. Always smiling. Always willing to help."

"Boyfriend? Anyone who paid her too much attention at the diner?" His pencil poised over the notebook. Someone had to know something.

"I can't think of anyone." She wiped away another tear. "Do you think those people could've killed her? I promise not to ever serve them again."

"They could have, but it doesn't feel right. Don't anger them." This woman was a favorite of Misty Hollow. If anything happened to her, there'd be a war. "Think real hard, Lucy. Maybe something Amber said that could give us a clue?"

"No, your best bet for anything personal would be Heather. The two spent a lot of time together outside of work."

"Thank you. Please send her over." He was getting nowhere.

A pale, sobbing young woman slid across from him. "I'm Heather."

He smiled, trying to put her at ease. "I'd like to ask you a few questions, if that's all right."

"Okay." She stared at the wadded tissue in her hands.

He repeated the same questions he'd asked the chef and Lucy. When he brought up the subject of a boyfriend, she jerked her head up. "Yeah. Her boyfriend, Lance, is here. Well, she said she was going to break up with him after breakfast. He's sitting over there. The guy alone."

Joey glanced over to where a dark-skinned man in his mid-twenties sat staring at his folded hands.

"Deputy, you might want to see this." Buster jerked his head toward the back of the diner.

Joey excused himself and followed the man down the short hall leading to the back door.

Buster opened the door to the men's bathroom. "There's a bit of blood in one of the stalls and another drop near the sink. Whoever killed that girl was in this room. Might still be in the diner."

"I need to take a look at people's shoes. Want to take half the room while I do the other?"

"Absolutely."

"Try to be inconspicuous. I'm going to talk to the victim's boyfriend." Joey headed to the table where the boyfriend sat and pulled out a chair. "Lance, I'm Deputy Hudson. I've heard you know the victim well."

"She's my girlfriend." He barely spoke above a whisper, his eyes averted.

"I'm sorry for your loss. Mind if I ask you a few questions?"

"Go ahead."

Joey nudged his pencil off the table with his elbow. "Excuse me." He bent to retrieve the pencil and studied the man's shoes. Along the side of the sole, he spotted a smear of blood. Writing implement in hand, he straightened.

As soon as his gaze met Lance's, the other man shot to his feet and darted toward the door.

Joey stood. "Stop him!"

Two diners stepped in front of the door.

Buster raced across the room and launched himself at Lance, tackling the man to the ground. "Got him." He pinned Lance to the ground.

The two FBI agents pulled him to his feet and faced Joey, a question on both their faces.

"There's blood on his shoe. I bet it'll match the victim's." Which meant the Robertos did not kill her. "Why?" He narrowed his eyes.

"It wasn't planned." The man heaved a sigh. "I joined her for breakfast on her break. She broke up with me. When I saw her head for the alley with the garbage, I followed her to try and talk her into not breaking things off." He pulled a cell phone from his pocket. "When I caught her giggling on this, I lost it. I thought it was another man, but it wasn't. She was talking to one of her girlfriends. So, I picked up the nearest thing I could find, an iron bar, and hit her with it."

"Where's the bar?"

"Over the fence. It'll have my prints all over it."

Joey had the FBI agents hand the man over to the deputies and haul him to the station. "Fast move, Buster."

"Yeah, I'm too old for such things. Ready to head back?"

"More than ready." His head pounded, and exhaustion slowed his movements. He sagged against the nearest table and willed the dizziness to pass.

Buster grabbed his shoulder and helped him to a seat. "You stay right there. I'll get Delly."

~

Jessica stared at the long line of motorcycles cruising past the house for the third time that day. It was obvious they weren't going away. "The town is crawling with cowboys on horses."

One of her mother's goons, Anthony—at least that's what Jessica thought his name was—cleaned his fingernails with a pocketknife. "It's kind of weird."

They'd become prisoners. "Where's my mother?"

"Napping."

"Wake her up and tell her I need to talk to her."

"No can do. I don't take orders from you."

"I'm here." Her mother entered and sat on the sofa and crossed her ankles. "There's no sleeping with the rumble of those motorcycles. What are they doing?"

"Driving back and forth." Jessica planted her fists on her hips. "Anthony said the town is crawling with cowboys patrolling the streets. We can't do anything from this house, so we need to relocate."

"This is a small town." Her mother tilted her head. "Where do you suggest we go?"

"Anywhere that allows us to leave the house and do our business. I've not had nearly enough time to bring this town to its knees." Killing a couple of homeless people did nothing more than make the Coopers nervous. It didn't make the sheriff and his deputies come crawling to her.

"There is nowhere to go but back to New York. Even that will be difficult, but since they have no real evidence you've done anything wrong, we might manage."

"Not New York. There's bound to be a place close enough to Misty Hollow for me to complete my plans." She chewed on a fingernail that desperately needed a manicure. Her mind flitted from one idea to another. They needed all the attention of law enforcement to be focused on one place in order to take their eyes off her and her mother long enough for them to move. The man who had failed to dispose of the deputy was now expendable enough to order to do the job.

She marched into the kitchen. "Rick, I need you to cause enough trouble at the Cooper home to keep the sheriff focused there."

"Okay. How?"

"Make yourself a nuisance. Just don't kill them. Not yet. I don't have my money."

"That sounds like a suicide mission, Boss."

Jessica left the room to the sound of him calling her name. Each time the desperation in the man's voice grew. He knew he was dead whether he followed orders or didn't. She grinned and headed to her room to pack.

# Chapter Twenty-One

**Buster, having declared** he would be spending the night since Joey wasn't much use to anyone in his opinion, spread blankets on the living room floor. "I'll sleep better down here than in a chair, recliner or not."

Mom planted her fists on her hips, started to argue, then snapped her mouth closed and headed to the kitchen, muttering something about coffee and fools.

Delly sent an amused glance at the men. "Coffee is her answer for everything."

Dani plopped into the chair Buster refused. Her eyes darted from one face to the other, then settled on Delly.

Uh-oh. Delly recognized the silent communication of her twin. The plan was going down tonight, and Dani was terrified. She gave a nod, letting her sister know she agreed to be a part of it. After all that had happened, with no sign of things improving, she'd do everything she could to help put an end to it all.

The hardest part would be sneaking away from the men. If she could convince Joey to take a pain med, he'd be out like a light, and they could escape out the back. She dug the bottle of pills from her purse.

"I'm not taking those." Joey settled on the sofa. "I need to stay alert."

"You need the rest. Buster is here to watch over us."

"No." He crossed his arms. The look on his face clearly said the conversation was over.

Stubborn man. She dropped the bottle back into her bag and joined her mother in the kitchen. "I have no idea how we're going to get out of here."

"I do." She sprinkled white powder into two of the coffee cups.

"Drugging people is illegal, Mom." Delly frowned.

"It's sleeping pills, not a drug." She dumped in sugar and stirred. "I simply mixed up their coffee with my own."

"That won't work." She tossed her hands up. "We're going to be arrested."

"If you would've stayed in the other room, you'd be none the wiser."

Good grief. They'd all be behind bars if they lived through this. Not wanting to see more, Delly returned to the living room as Mother handed out the drinks. Her mouth filled with cotton, and she set her mug on the coffee table untouched. Eyes wide, she watched as the two men sipped their drinks.

"Who wants to watch TV?" Mom picked up the remote. "I'm sure we're all too wound up to go to sleep right now."

How could she act as if she hadn't just committed a crime? As if she, Delly, and Dani weren't about to risk their lives enticing a cold-blooded killer into the open? Their lives were worth more than fifteen-thousand dollars, weren't they? What made her think she was brave enough to do this?

Joey's eyes narrowed as he looked at her. Then, a look of betrayal crossed his face. "What did you do?" His words slurred.

"She didn't do anything. It was all me. Now lie back, and let us—"

The front window shattered.

Dani screamed and leaped from the chair, then fell, clutching her foot.

Delly hit the floor.

Mom ducked behind a chair.

Buster tried to stand and failed. "We've been drugged, Joey." His eyes rolled back in his head, and he crashed onto the blankets on the floor.

Joey's eyes were already closed.

A rock lay in the middle of the room, a sheet of paper wrapped around it.

Delly crawled over and unwrapped the paper. "*Let's have some fun.*" Her blood chilled. "They're here." She glared at her mother. "And you've successfully taken out our protection."

"Come on." She grabbed a backpack from behind the sofa. "Let's get this over with."

"You can't leave me." Dani still held her foot. "I've broken something."

"For crying out loud!" Mom heaved a sigh. "Can't anything go as planned?"

Footsteps pounded across the front porch. Another window shattered. Sirens wailed in the distance.

"Good. Help is coming. The instant they pull into the drive, you and me will head out the back. Got it?" She pierced Delly with her gaze.

She nodded, regretting her decision to go along

with the plan. "With the authorities here, you'll be fine, Dani."

"But what about you and Mom? It's me they want."

"Then, I'll be you." She pulled her hair from its ponytail and grabbed her sister's well-worn coat. "Mom will call once we've lured Jessica out in the open. That's when you send help. You know the place." Since the campground was virtually empty during the winter, they'd decided to head in that direction.

Tears spilled down her sister's face. "Somehow, I'll make this up to you, sis. I promise."

"All I need is for you to call for help."

Flashing lights shone through the broken window. With one last tender look at Joey, Delly sprinted out the back door, praying it wasn't the last time she'd lay eyes on him. The hurt expression on his face had ripped at her heart. There would be a lot of explaining to do when this was all over.

Mom had parked on the next street over. "I'm going to drop you off on the highway. We need you to be out there long enough for someone to spot you. If that doesn't work, call this number before entering the campgrounds." She handed Delly a ripped piece of paper.

Two numbers were on the slip, one crossed out and one circled. The crossed out one had to be the father's. Delly would rather deal with him than his daughter and the mother. Both women seemed far worse in her opinion. And, here she was, about to call them to come for her. Both she and her mother were certifiably insane.

Her mother stopped two miles from the

campground and parked in the trees. "I'm thinking they might have a tracker on your sister's pack, but just in case, we have the phone number. I have my gun in my purse. You'll never be out of my sight. If things get ugly and the sheriff's men are late, I'll start shooting."

"Great. I'll be caught in the crossfire." She shoved her door open.

"I thought you wanted to end this before more people die."

"I do, but I don't have to like it." She closed the door and stared at her mother over the top. "I love you, Mom."

"I love you, too, sweetie. Now, go. Night has fallen, and it's cold and foggy out here. Fitting for such an adventure, don't you think?"

Delly's heart beat so hard in her throat she was surprised her mother didn't hear. "See you later." She slung the backpack over her shoulders. Hands in her pockets, hood up and head down, she headed for the campground.

The fog muffled the sound of her boots on the asphalt. No birds twittered from the trees. No headlights pierced the fog. She felt more alone than she had ever felt in her life.

The sign to the campground came into view. It didn't look as if Jessica's men were coming. Delly pulled the phone from her pocket and dialed the number.

"Yeah?"

"This is…Dani. I have the rest of your money, and I'm at the Misty Hollow campground by the second bathroom."

The line was silent for a moment. "How did you

know we weren't at the house?"

They weren't? She'd had no idea. "Well, I have my ways. I learned a lot from your father." Please, believe the lie.

"Who's with you?"

"I'm alone. Are you coming or not? It's cold out here."

"I'm coming." Jessica hung up.

Delly ducked into the bathroom. Since it was the off season, no one had turned on the heater, and the place was only marginally warmer than outside. She sent her mother a text that the call had been made.

I have the bathroom in sight. Good job. It's almost over.

Fifteen minutes later, the sound of tires, then doors slamming drew Delly from the bathroom. She stepped under a streetlamp as Jessica and her mother stood near a black Cadillac. In the driver's seat sat a man whose face she couldn't see.

Her heart started galloping again as she removed the pack from her back. She had no idea whether it held the other fifteen-thousand or not. If not, things could end very quickly. Instead of helping her daughter, Mom would watch her daughter be gunned down. She took a couple of steps forward and dropped the pack.

"Bring it closer," Stephanie said. "We want to make sure you're alone."

"I said I was." She picked the bag back up and moved a few steps closer. The man in the vehicle turned to stare. The streetlight outside the bathroom illuminated his face. She frowned. He looked familiar. Where had she...oh.

His eyes widened, and he shook his head. One of

the FBI agents had gone undercover. How had he infiltrated the other side so soon? Or had he infiltrated the FBI?

Jessica's eyes narrowed. She reached her hand into her pocket.

The agent shoved his door open, a gun in his hand. "Down, Miss Cooper."

A bullet ripped through the side of Dani's coat as Jessica fired. Delly dropped to the ground as both Roberto women started shooting.

The agent dashed to the other side of the car and continued shooting.

Delly crawled on her stomach toward the bathroom.

"I don't think so." Mrs. Roberto grabbed her hood and yanked her to her feet before using Delly as a shield. The woman's hand shook.

Jessica lay unmoving near the vehicle.

The agent aimed his weapon over the top of the car. "Put down the gun."

"I can't do that." Stephanie backed toward the building.

Delly's mother stepped from the trees. "Get your hands off my daughter."

Stephanie turned.

Delly slammed an elbow into the woman's ribs. She gasped and squeezed the trigger, her shot going wild. The agent fired again, dropping her.

Seconds later, Sheriff Westbrook and two other deputies skidded to a halt behind the Cadillac. "Where's Deputy Hudson?" He shot a quick look at Delly.

"Mom put a sleeping pill in both his and Buster's

coffee. They're home sleeping it off." She sagged against her mother. "You are the most amazing woman I've ever met."

Mom hugged her, then retrieved the backpack. "Glad I still have my money. Are you okay?"

Delly nodded. "Dani is going to need a new parka." She poked her finger through the bullet hole in the side of the coat. "Good thing it's a size too large."

If looks could kill, the sheriff's eyes would have burned them both to a crisp. "We'll talk about drugging a law enforcement officer in the morning. I expect both of you at the station by nine."

"We'll be there." Mom shrugged. "I doubt I'll get jail time. Not much anyway."

Despite the seriousness of the situation, Delly spewed out a guffaw—a deep laugh that came from the belly. One that released all the fear and tension of the last few weeks.

"Let's go home before you completely lose your mind." Her mother put an arm around Delly's waist and led her back to the car.

# Chapter Twenty-Two

A very irate Joey stood over Delly's bed the next morning. "You have some 'splaining to do."

Blinking, she sat up. "It was all my mother. I'm so sorry."

"You could've been killed, Delly." He dropped to his knees. "I wouldn't have survived that."

She cupped his cheek. "That's exactly how I felt when I heard you were attacked while fighting that fire. It's over now, Joey."

"It's coming up on nine o'clock, and the sheriff texted me that I'd better have you and your mother there precisely at nine."

She stretched. "Okay. Give me five minutes."

Twenty minutes later, at 9:05, Delly and her mother sat across from Joey and the sheriff in the conference room. The case board still displayed all the pieces of the Robertos' reign.

The sheriff slid an envelope across the table. "This was in Jessica Roberto's pocket."

The envelope contained Delly's check. "She didn't cash it."

"For whatever reason." He folded his hands on the tabletop. "Now, to the crime you committed."

"*I* committed." Mom smiled and tilted her head. "Delly had nothing to do with me slipping the sleeping pills in Joey and Buster's coffee. I did so, because I knew it was the only way we'd be able to get out of the house. Whoever threw that rock in the window provided us with the perfect opportunity." She looked pleased with herself.

Delly met Joey's gaze. The soft look on his face said he'd forgiven her. She smiled and relaxed.

"It's against the law, Mrs. Cooper."

"I'm aware of that, Sheriff. But, as a mother, it was more important to me that my daughters were safe. Which they are. That is worth whatever punishment the court system dishes out."

He shook his head. "I don't think I've ever met anyone like you, and to be frank, ma'am, I hope I never do again."

"Jessica Roberto died from gunshot wounds." Joey sat back in his chair. "Her mother is in the hospital in critical condition."

"And the agent?" Delly really hoped he'd made it out alive.

"Uninjured."

She lowered her head. "It's my fault the shooting started. I recognized him from one of the times he came into the diner, and I couldn't keep the surprise off my face." Thankfully, she wouldn't have the guilt of his death on her conscience.

The sheriff said Mom had to appear in court in ten days but told her she'd most likely get probation rather than jail time because of the circumstances. He pushed to his feet. "Do you plan on staying in town, Mrs. Cooper?"

"I haven't decided yet but most likely."

"Lord, help us all."

Joey escorted them out and pulled Delly off to the side. "I have to stay and finish a few things, but I have to know…are you staying?"

She could drown in his eyes. "Do you want me to?"

"More than anything." He leaned his forehead against hers. "I want to see where the future takes us. You and me. I want to spend time with you when we aren't in danger. I want to do all the things normal people do when they're dating."

"That sounds wonderful to me. There's nothing for me in Texarkana, although there is one more thing I want to do before I close this chapter on my life. Will you meet me at the lake tonight? Six o'clock?"

"Anything you want." He caressed her cheek. "See you then."

At six o'clock, Delly waited by her truck full of brand-new tents, sleeping bags, propane heaters, and gas stoves. Nothing felt better than using the money Jessica hadn't cashed toward helping the people who had lost everything.

When Joey arrived, the line stretched a hundred yards out. His gaze lit up as they settled on her. "You are a remarkable woman, Delaney Cooper. We can date for as long as you want, but I already know our future holds a wedding with you becoming my wife."

"Is that a proposal?" She smiled.

"Maybe."

"If it is, I say yes." She handed the next person the things they needed to start anew. "I think you should at least give me a kiss when you propose."

"Gladly." He cupped her face and lowered his head.

## The End

Coming early fall, A Place to Hide in ebook form. Already available in print.

www.cynthiahickey.com

Cynthia Hickey is a multi-published and best-selling author of cozy mysteries and romantic suspense. She has taught writing at many conferences and small writing retreats. She and her husband run the publishing press, Winged Publications. They live in Arizona and Arkansas, becoming snowbirds with three dogs. They have ten grandchildren who keep them busy and tell everyone they know that "Nana is a writer."

**Misty Hollow**
Secrets of Misty Hollow
Deceptive Peace
Calm Surface
Lightning Never Strikes Twice
Lethal Inheritance
Bitter Isolation
Say I Don't
Christmas Stalker
Bridge to Safety

Connect with me on FaceBook
Twitter
Sign up for my newsletter and receive a free short story
www.cynthiahickey.com

Follow me on Amazon
And Bookbub
   Shop my bookstore on shopify. For better price and autographed.

Enjoy other books by Cynthia Hickey

**Misty Hollow**
Secrets of Misty Hollow
Deceptive Peace
Calm Surface
Lightning Never Strikes Twice
Lethal Inheritance
Bitter Isolation
Say I Don't
Christmas Stalker
Bridge to Safety

   Stay in Misty Hollow for a while. Get the entire series here!

**The Seven Deadly Sins series**
Deadly Pride
Deadly Covet
Deadly Lust
Deadly Glutton
Deadly Envy
Deadly Sloth
Deadly Anger

## The Tail Waggin' Mysteries
Cat-Eyed Witness
The Dog Who Found a Body
Troublesome Twosome
Four-Legged Suspect
Unwanted Christmas Guest
Wedding Day Cat Burglar

## Brothers Steele
Sharp as Steele
Carved in Steele
Forged in Steele
Brothers Steele (All three in one)

## The Brothers of Copper Pass
Wyatt's Warrant
Dirk's Defense
Stetson's Secret
Houston's Hope
Dallas's Dare
Seth's Sacrifice
Malcolm's Misunderstanding
The Brothers of Copper Pass Boxed Set

## Time Travel
The Portal

## Tiny House Mysteries
No Small Caper
Caper Goes Missing
Caper Finds a Clue

Caper's Dark Adventure
A Strange Game for Caper
Caper Steals Christmas
Caper Finds a Treasure
Tiny House Mysteries boxed set

## Wife for Hire – Private Investigators
Saving Sarah
Lesson for Lacey
Mission for Meghan
Long Way for Lainie
Aimed at Amy
Wife for Hire (all five in one)

## A Hollywood Murder
Killer Pose, book 1
Killer Snapshot, book 2
Shoot to Kill, book 3
Kodak Kill Shot, book 4
To Snap a Killer
Hollywood Murder Mysteries

## Shady Acres Mysteries
Beware the Orchids, book 1
Path to Nowhere
Poison Foliage
Poinsettia Madness
Deadly Greenhouse Gases
Vine Entrapment
Shady Acres Boxed Set

## CLEAN BUT GRITTY Romantic Suspense

## Highland Springs

Murder Live
Say Bye to Mommy
To Breathe Again
Highland Springs Murders (all 3 in one)

## Colors of Evil Series

Shades of Crimson
Coral Shadows

## The Pretty Must Die Series

Ripped in Red, book 1
Pierced in Pink, book 2
Wounded in White, book 3
Worthy, The Complete Story

## Lisa Paxton Mystery Series

Eenie Meenie Miny Mo
Jack Be Nimble
Hickory Dickory Dock
Boxed Set

Hearts of Courage
A Heart of Valor
The Game
Suspicious Minds
After the Storm

Local Betrayal
Hearts of Courage Boxed Set

Overcoming Evil series
Mistaken Assassin
Captured Innocence
Mountain of Fear
Exposure at Sea
A Secret to Die for
Collision Course
Romantic Suspense of 5 books in 1

## INSPIRATIONAL

### Nosy Neighbor Series
Anything For A Mystery, Book 1
A Killer Plot, Book 2
Skin Care Can Be Murder, Book 3
Death By Baking, Book 4
Jogging Is Bad For Your Health, Book 5
Poison Bubbles, Book 6
A Good Party Can Kill You, Book 7
Nosy Neighbor collection

Christmas with Stormi Nelson

### The Summer Meadows Series
Fudge-Laced Felonies, Book 1
Candy-Coated Secrets, Book 2
Chocolate-Covered Crime, Book 3
Maui Macadamia Madness, Book 4

CYNTHIA HICKEY

All four novels in one collection

**The River Valley Mystery Series**
Deadly Neighbors, Book 1
Advance Notice, Book 2
The Librarian's Last Chapter, Book 3
All three novels in one collection

Made in the USA
Middletown, DE
14 February 2024

49763237R00104